CW00404574

THE DIRT AND THE STARS

Robert

Cowan

Copyright 2018 Robert Cowan

Cover design: Robert Cowan

Editing/proofing: Stephanie Dagg

All characters portrayed herein are entirely fictional. Any resemblance to any person living, dead, or anywhere in between for that matter, is entirely coincidental.

ALSO BY ROBERT COWAN:

THE SEARCH FOR ETHAN
DAYDREAMS AND DEVILS
FOR ALL IS VANITY
FIRM

Dedicated to:

Carol, Keith and Fern.

My Stars Amongst the Dirt

Acknowledgements

Big thanks to the following for Beta / Proof reading:

Kevin Berg
Claire Carroll
Gordon Cowan
Shervin Jamali
Gayle Robertson Karabelen
Nicola Kinney
Mari McCrossan
Keith Nixon
Elaine Lyness Ramsay
Tracy Stewart

CHAPTER 1

The girl shivered, pressing her eyes firmly closed to keep the truth at bay. But she didn't need eyes to see the icy water seep down through the bridge's sandstone pillars, eroding the gang's graffiti just as the winter had their fair-weather bravado. She heard the last of the leaves fall in the wind, having held out before joining the others piled up beneath, covering coils of dog shit, the remains of fires and late-night parties, beer cans buckled and glass shattered into the diamonds of bums. Dust turned to mud, seeping like the earth's blood, drying as scars in the cracked cement. What sensory gaps there were, her nose filled in, though most had been mercifully washed away by the cleansing rain. But there the mercy ended. Because you can see with your eyes closed. You can feel the damp of the earth and of the air and of your breath with your eyes closed. You can dream, remember and hear the echoes of nightmares with your eyes closed. And you can cry with your eyes closed.

Inevitably Mary opened them, taking a second to adjust. She glanced down; the eyes of Carnation looked back with what seemed like love. Mary squeezed the pink kitten, finding comfort in its softness, nourishment in its textiles, kissing her head as she placed her gently in the rucksack, wrapped in her blanket.

As she stood, Mary looked around as a tourist might at the end of their holiday, soaking up the details. Remembering. A sad farewell to what had been their home. But any flickers of nostalgia were quickly snuffed out. The world was getting cold. She had to move to better shelter.

CHAPTER 2

There are a few times in life when you question your sanity. I've never been married so I've been spared that particular spite-fuelled cauldron and the pus-spurting ecstasy of divorce. I have, however, just moved house and that is as close to madness's pinnacle as I ever wish to reach. The hunt for the perfect home, the despondent settling for something that'll do, estate agents and solicitors, two sides of the same back-scratching coin, hustling in an ethical no man's land through which the chain of buyers and sellers must shuffle while constantly listening for the whistle of sniper fire as they and their cardboard boxes are conveyed all of two miles to 52 Waste of Time Avenue, which looks pretty much like where they just left, with the addition of one bedroom in which no one will sleep and will soon be referred to as 'storage', perfect for the boxes they brought with them full of stuff that may see the light of day once more over the coming weeks and months before joining the charity shop run.

I didn't have a house warming party.

The neighbours popped round earlier. Fred and Samantha. Mid-thirties, so we had that in common. Christ could she talk. Lips like a hummingbird's wings. Quite flirty though. They didn't stay long. It was probably more of a 'brief spying mission then compare notes back home' sort of thing. I wasn't too sure about him. Looked shifty as fuck. One eyebrow, that's the giveaway. Probably a used car salesman.

I looked over to the clock. Seven-thirty seemed a reasonable time for the first beer on a Friday night. Pity it was Wednesday, but fuck it, seven-thirty is seven-thirty, when you no longer have work to question the toxicity of your breath, whether you had arrived by bus and why you had arrived at all. After a thorough search of the cutlery drawer, I remembered the bottle opener was in one of the boxes, but which one? Sadly not one marked 'bottle opener'. Bottled beer does taste better, but cans don't need a bottle opener. Difficult decisions lay ahead.

I counted twenty-two boxes in total. Bottle opener? Box twenty-one. So now I'd got a thirst like I'd spent five days in the Sahara licking stale Ryvitas. On the plus side, when I did finally pop that first bottle...for just a few seconds it was like all of life's misery had been washed away in an oral baptism of sweet sweet beer. The rest never quite match the peak refreshment of number one, but it's UnFriday night and I was settling in for a *Better Call Saul* marathon. The doorbell chimed. I sighed, though it came out as "Fuck's sake." I thought about ignoring it before the second chime, and it is a truly irritating chime, forced me to my feet. I opened the door to find Samantha again in all her red-haired, voluptuous splendour on the top step. We were eyeball to eyeball and chest to

4

chest as the gravitational pull of her vast, earth mother bosom drew me closer. She smiled. The beer egged me on so I smiled back. She seemed to like that. I noticed the scent of wine on her breath and wanted to kiss her, but before I could.

"Go ahead and ask him," yelled Fred, out of sight, lurking in his hallway.

"Shut up, for fuck's sake, I was just going to!" she slurred with a loud belch.

The wine wasn't smelling so sexy now.

Her invisible partner turned the volume up. "We're missing *Big Brother*!"

"Pause it then! Jesus H Christ. What's he like, eh? Gets worked up over nothing." She moved a little closer. "And what gets you worked up, eh?" she winked.

Before I could answer, Fred bellowed again, "We're having a barbecue tomorrow. Get yer arse round about seven. Samantha, get your arse round now, looks like Tony's getting kicked out."

"Better fucking not, he's my favourite!" she moaned to her husband before turning back. "See you tomorrow night. "

Only a half wink this time as she rushed back to find out Tony's fate. Actually, she may have a squint.

I sat back down and lit a cigarette, pondering whether I would go or not, but quickly realising that sometimes you have no choice and this was one of those. Resigned, I switched over to *Big Brother* just in time to see Tony get his marching orders, probably heading straight to the tanning salon from the look of him. I was sure I could hear Samantha wail through the wall. Stubbing out the cigarette I flicked back to *Better Call Saul* and other than the taking on and passing of fluids, stayed there for the next four hours watching Jimmy and Mike and thinking of tomorrow's wallpaper stripping.

Funny how little things can change your life.

CHAPTER 3

The next morning I woke mercifully hangover-free, yet feeling that heaviness of mind and waning spirit that were the calling card of depression. It'd been a while but I knew I needed to nip this fucker in the bud. With an anxious sigh I forced myself out of bed, tensing my face muscles to wring some energy in or maybe to squeeze the demons out, but hopefully no one was walking past the window as, from the look on my face, they would no doubt have concluded my hands weren't idle but the Devil's work was being done.

I made some strong coffee, two heaped spoons with a good shot of milk to smooth the bitterness out. Turning the TV on I scanned through channel after channel of mind-skewering shit. Off. But I needed to do something. More coffee brought the jitters. I thought I had this behind me. I pushed it to the side and remembered the wallpaper stripping plans I'd made for the morning. A trivial, mundane task that now seemed absurdly overwhelming. But I knew I had to try. The alternative, if given time to sprout, would be unbearable. When I was young I was convinced that DIY was itself a mental illness linked in some mysterious way to public holidays. The Easter bunny, patron saint of power tools drawing his followers to the church of B&Q. But now here it was, revealed as my therapy, my saviour. Christ, what a depressing thought.

Soon the steamer, still peppered with paper and paste from the last campaign, was gurgling and ready for action once again. But I was not. I left it for a few minutes to fill the bedroom with steam then thought about stripping off my clothes and having a sauna instead. But I hate saunas even more than DIY, so I picked up the steamer tool and pressed it firmly over the first rectangle of wallpaper, next to the door frame with its nice straight edge, then moved up piece by piece, ignoring the voice in my head almost chanting 'Can't be arsed. Can't be arsed. Can't be arsed,' over and over to the tune of 'Here we go'. I really couldn't be arsed. Only when I was convinced the paper would offer no resistance did I move to the scraper, starting again at the bottom, delivering short stabbing thrusts to the surrendering enemy and the Geneva Convention. Christ, I couldn't be arsed but I continued anyway until, removing some paper, some writing was revealed.

'Mary aged 2' next to a horizontal line. I pictured a smiling little girl standing unsteadily as her dad recorded a little piece of family history. I pictured his own smile, his pride, then my sadness, a sadness for opportunities missed, maybe lost. I thought of a beer but knew now was definitely the wrong time. So I carried on, soon coming across 'Mary aged 3…4…5' and so on until '9'. On and on I scraped, searching, but Mary was gone. Maybe she'd grown too old for such childish nonsense? Or perhaps she'd moved to another house, now home to Mary aged 10…11? Maybe her mum and dad had divorced and Mary was now alone with a mother with no interest in perpetuating this reminder of the man who had cheated on her, tossed her aside for a younger model, a prettier model, maybe just a dirtier model. But he could rot in hell, and anyway, she could see how big Mary was. She had eyes. Prick!

With my mind calmed down, I soldiered on through the paper, which surrendered as easily as an Italian tank battalion on a rainy day. I was half-way through the third wall and the second beer, feeling pretty good about the world, when Mary came knocking, walking straight in, inviting questions but keeping her secrets. What age would she be now? Where is she? What did she look like?

I put the scraper down as I pondered, unconsciously walking to the fridge and opening another breakfast beer. Morning drinking, when any dregs of dignity are hacked into the spittoon of full-blown alcoholism. I looked at the clock in the corner. 12:03. There, I was now cloaked in the relative respectability of afternoon drinking, not that I cared too much, which is just as well as I remembered I hadn't changed the clocks since they went back. 11:03 it is.

Just as I was about to start on the last wall, the adjoining wall, the noises started. First a sound like a cornered feral cat. Then a car crash victim enmeshed in twisted metal, drizzled in diesel ready to ignite, screaming in pain, begging for release until, finally, a gasp like a woman dragged from the sea seconds from drowning. I glanced back at the clock. 11:06. Efficient. Assuming this was Mary's room, had she had to endure next door's erotic wailings at all hours like some CIA-sponsored Psych Warfare Program? I pictured Mary, headphones clamped tight, praying to the gods of S Club 7 to make it go away. Is that why she moved? The whole household must have heard. The whole fucking street must have heard. But maybe Fred and Samantha weren't the 'tone it down, please' types. Maybe Mary's family decided they'd had enough and they just decided…Fuck me, they were at it again!

I called a halt, switched off the steamer and retired to the living room, closing every door behind me on the way. Then I turned up the TV…Bit more…Christ, she was sounding like Bruce Lee now. It was going to be hard to look her in the eye tonight. Squint or no squint.

CHAPTER 4

Next door, Samantha thanked God for Duracell batteries as she wiped off the vibrator and tossed it back into the open drawer. Alone in the king-size bed she stretched out, naked, enjoying the freedom, smiling as she considered round three. But she was sure she'd gotten her message across. She got up, walked to the en-suite bathroom, stepping over her comatose husband on the way, and turned on the shower, immersing herself under her own little waterfall just on the side of nipple swelling cold. She closed her eyes and imagined…Usually Daniel Craig.

"Fuck it."

The echo from the tiles amplified her wailings as her husband slept and when she'd finished she did her crying in the rain.

In the kitchen she waited for the kettle to boil, shivering as the silk robe hugged the still wet small of her back. She pulled it closed, feeling both robe and loneliness tighten and follow her as she wandered over to the window to watch two blue tits pecking away at the lone bird feeder. She watched a while as she sipped her coffee, thoughts drifting to her new neighbour. He was no Daniel Craig, but with a similar hair style, height and blue eyes, handsome at a more attainable level, and given the soulless state of her marriage definitely a catch. He seemed nice too. Hopefully not too nice.

Jolted from her daydreams by the sound of her husband retching, she sighed and drained her coffee, torn between another mug and something stronger but her husband was a poor advert for alcohol. Another retch and she headed for the percolator. She looked over as he entered the kitchen, his smile revealing more post-vomit debris than affection. Samantha's wince didn't go unnoticed.

"You're not looking too 'Bond girl' yourself, sweetheart."

She turned away.

"What? Am I just too real for you? You used to like that as I remember."

"That was a long time ago, before.."

"Well fucking thanks for that."

Samantha pointed at the percolator. "Drink some of that and sober up."

"Christ, you've got a cheek."

The next few hours passed in a simmering casserole of game show repeats, junk food, loud flatulence and silent contempt, all wrapped in a brick and mortar shroud whose décor was two decades out of date. But slowly, Samantha began to emerge, her thoughts turning to the barbecue, a chance for fun and who knows what else... The barbecue!

"The barbecue! Fuck, we've nothing in!"

"We're not really doing that, are we?"

"It was your fucking idea!"

"I know but I was pissed."

"You're always pissed! We're doing it. I'm not spending Sat-"

"Right! Right! For Christ's sake. At least I'll have other people to drink with."

"Let's go. Tesco. No, Sainsbury's. It's a special occasion."

"What special occasion?"

"New neighbours."

"What? Are we having a street party now? We'll break out the bunting, shall we?"

Samantha shook her head. "Just get your shoes on and let's go."

"You go. I can't be arsed."

"You're a lazy cunt. I don't know what you want."

Fred shook his glass. "Same again, bartender."

CHAPTER 5

The salt and vinegar of the crisps nipped her cracked lips as Mary walked towards the city centre. She was young, but just old enough to hide in plain sight amongst the passing pedestrians whose only thoughts were getting to work in time for a cup of coffee, the horror of the hours to follow suppressed until caffeine made them manageable. She walked eyes down lest any accidental eye contact should trigger concern, questions or the need to intervene. There could be no risk of that. On she walked, matching speed with the human traffic, blending, not knowing where she was going but certain she would know it.

Up ahead Mary saw a convenience store and searched her memory, wondering if she'd been there before, if so when, and had she burned her bridges? But she found nothing. She slowed her pace until she saw others enter and followed behind. The shop was busy, so easy to hide in. Mulling amongst the morning rush she found the fridge. A man opened it, took what he needed then held it open. She took the door handle silently with a polite nod of thanks as he turned and walked to the till. She felt her heart beat hard in her chest once again as she struggled to breath, pausing, but only for a second. Quickly, she lifted two litres of milk and a chunk of cheese, tucked them inside her coat, then, placing a large lady between herself and the till, headed to the exit. All her attention was focussed on her hearing at these moments, when danger was at its peak, listening for any hint of disruption. Out on the street, moving further and further away, she looked around checking for escape routes, gaps between pedestrians, careful to move only her eyes, her head fixed forward, unremarkable. In her head she counted. Ten…twenty…fear falling as the numbers rose…fifty…At sixty she felt safe.

After a while she came across a park, small, fenced off from the world and littered with the remnants of autumn. After a brief tour she selected a bench located in a far corner and sufficiently obscured by bushes. There she sat alone with her hunger. She grasped the block of cheese in her small, numb fingers and gnawed at the plastic till she had a hole big enough for a finger-nail, tearing further until it was big enough to bite off a piece. She chewed, savouring the rich flavour as she sat cut off from the world. Almost.

She tensed as a woman approached; thin, skin vacuum-packed tight on her bones, her eyes troubled, suffocating in their sockets, straining ahead, passing Mary by seemingly unnoticed. A few steps later the woman stopped, glancing back at her, their eyes connecting. Sensing there was nothing for her here she walked on to wherever her desperation, scab-littered arms and torn trainers led.

Mary watched frozen with a cold and fearful sympathy until the woman was out of sight. Then she opened the milk and drank great gulps; grateful for her quenching thirst, cursing its chill, but afraid to stop. Halfway through she sat the plastic bottle on the bench beside her, screwing on the top in case she spilled it in a moment's clumsiness. She looked at the cheese, already half finished. Desperate both to eat and to make it last she sat, nibbling her cheese like the mouse she was and looking for a hole in which to hide.

In the corner, some densely packed bushes caught her eye. Folding the plastic around the remaining cheese and tucking it into her pocket, she watched, waiting until she was sure the park was empty before approaching the bushes. With one last look she tunnelled her way through, happy that the ground was dry, as muddy children draw attention. Reaching the perimeter wall she stopped and looked back. The park was hidden. She smiled. This could be home for a time at least. She leaned back against the wall and ate the rest of the cheese.

CHAPTER 6

I never had her down as the Sainsbury's type. More Aldi, or Tesco at a push. I never had me down as a supermarket snob either, but there you go. She had one of the big trolleys too, looking like she had a big night planned. Then I remembered...Fuck! The barbecue! I'd totally forgotten and really couldn't be arsed. For some reason I followed her, maybe to give myself a reason to call off. Dodgy burgers, cheap supermarket beer...cable ties and lubricant. I felt like a rooky cop on his first undercover tail, desperate not to be made, hanging back a couple of trolley lengths watching the traffic for sudden stops. She moved nicely with the trace of a wiggle, but natural rather than some self-conscious attention-seeking strut. She stopped when she got to the fresh meat counter. Steaks. She was pushing the boat out. Suddenly she turned but thankfully looked past me, smiling. Then I remembered the squint. Bugger. But as she walked towards me it turned out some squints were sexy. Sharleen Spiteri just got bumped into second.

"Hi. What you doing here?" she asked

I resisted pointing out the obvious. "Just...you know." Which if she did she wouldn't be asking.

Small talk paused she played with her hair. I felt 'stirrings' and moved my basket.

"I hope you're still coming round?" she asked, with almost no attempt to mask the desperation in her voice or her eyes.

"Yeah, I've been looking forward to it," I lied, though I now sort of was.

She seemed to relax, a smile equal parts happiness and gratitude appearing through the makeup.

"Good, I have too. Are you bringing some one? I'd meant to say, because that would be okay."

"Na, just me. A threesome."

I was about to explain that's not what I meant but she laughed a wonderful 'Janis Joplin being tickled' kind of laugh. Aisle three stopped in its tracks but Samantha didn't care. She now had a party.

"I doubt it. Fred will have passed out by eight so it'll be just us."

She reached over and gave my arm a squeeze. I repositioned my basket.

"Fred a bit of a drinker?" I asked.

"I'm a bit of a drinker. I think you are too. Fred? He's just an arse. Anyway, I don't want to put you off."

"Two's a party, three's a crowd," I heard myself saying, cringing. "Speaking of drink, what should I bring?"

She screwed her face up as if I'd suggested bringing Boris Johnson as a plus one.

"Don't you dare bring a thing!"

"I have to bring a bottle of something."

"No, you don't."

18

"I'm not coming empty-handed so they might as well be full of something you like."

Another smile.

"I do like a brandy and Babycham on special occasions. I've got the brandy here, so you bring the Babycham."

"Samantha, there's no way on God's green earth I'm standing at the checkout pulling Babycham out of my basket."

I reached into her trolley and lifted out the bottle of brandy, glancing at the unfamiliar, obviously cheap brand and put it into my basket.

"Well, nothing else. I invited you, remember?"

"We'll see."

"No, Tom. Nothing. Promise?"

"Okay, okay I promise."

Ten minutes later, as I stood at the checkout staring in disbelief at the brandy and then the £62.99 on the till screen for the third time, I knew that would be one fucking promise I'd be keeping.

CHAPTER 7

For hours Mary sat until, alone with no distractions, her thoughts and her memories broke free. They soared, screamed and stabbed as she whimpered in the bushes before the physical pain of hunger returned to break the spell. She stretched as best she could to ease the aches of her young body before crawling back out to the light, with a pause to check for passers by. Satisfied, she stood up, pulling her rucksack up onto her weary shoulders and headed off in search of food once more.

Every day at these times she cursed her youth, wishing she was able to beg like the grown-ups who seemed able to fill their cups with money yet remain ignored by all but the occasional soul who wished to throw in some words of kindness with their change. But a child begging would draw the attention of the entire world, so to survive she must steal and scavenge, constantly on the move to stay free.

She walked on through the rain and the wind and the cold, her eyes darting from side to side. Hope warmed her heart as she saw some packaging on the pavement up ahead. It was a sandwich, less than half eaten. Blessed are those with big eyes, small stomachs and no concern for the environment for theirs is the gratitude of the hungry. Mary knelt before it, giving thanks as she pretended to tie the shoe-laces she didn't have before picking it up and eating as if she'd just put it down. Still seemingly fresh, its slight sogginess made it easier to chew. It tasted like chicken, waking her appetite further as she walked to the traffic lights up ahead. Then, noticing almost all the waiting cars were turning left, she followed them thinking they must have a reason.

The reason was two hundred yards down on the left. Tesco. A smile flickered on Mary's face and her pace quickened, the soles of her shoes slapping on the glistening wet pavement. As the cars scouted out the best parking spots she made her way to the entrance and waited. Her stomach growled but still she waited and watched. A middle-aged man, smartly dressed, probably in sales. Another man, younger and rougher, glanced at her as he passed. Then a woman on her own, brown hair yanked back in a ponytail wearing a washed out blue fleece and jodhpurs pushing a trolley, one of the smaller ones. Then another woman, a young mother, dressed with casual elegance, eyes tired, stressed, toddler perched on the full-sized trolley, young eyes filled with wonder and mischief looking everywhere at once. As they entered, Mary tucked in behind them before setting her distance.

At the very first aisle Mary almost wept with Christmas morning joy at the sign in front of her, before composing herself and taking a banana from the basket marked 'Free fruit for children'.

Then an apple. As her hand reached for a tangerine she stopped it, instinctively sensing the attention it might draw. Biting into the apple, she tucked the banana in her pocket before walking quickly to catch up with her mother and baby sister, following behind, keeping to that blurred distance and careful to keep out of mum's view whenever possible.

The dairy section. A one-litre carton of full fat milk, refreshment and nourishment, emptied in the camera blind spot then deposited at the back of the first available shelf. Two cereal bars. They taste like cardboard but fill you up, and with the wrappers disposed of in mum's trolley not stolen, just hidden for now by a large box of cornflakes, Kellogg's, not 'own brand'. Mum only bought the best for her children. She could pay for the bars at the checkout.

Her 'baby sister' caught her eye, smiling and curious. Mary smiled back but turned away as mum looked to see where her baby was looking. Mum saw the back of a girl's head and continued shopping without missing a step. Mary breathed again, shuddering at first, then smoothly, calmly, as she had so many times before.

And on she followed, unnoticed, (having learned that for most grow-ups other people's children were usually a source of irritation and to be avoided), eating and invisible until finally they reached the checkout. That was the moment for Mary to point to the toilet, moving quickly before she had an accident, as mum, unaware, loaded the conveyor, picking up the empty wrappers with a confused look before tossing them back in the trolley as the rubbish they must be. Meanwhile, Mary locked the cubicle door, at first waiting, then just sitting. She took her shoes and socks off and rubbed the feeling back into her toes, still numb with cold. Then her jeans, sitting in the warmth and letting it soak into her skin, her flesh, bones and blood. She sat for a long, long time and wished it could be forever.

Footsteps came and went. Some to use, some to clean, some for reasons she didn't understand. When the cleaner returned a second time Mary knew her time was used up. She opened her eyes, rubbing them gently, then, as they adjusted to the harsh blue fluorescence, she flushed, dressed and slid back the snib. The cleaner smiled without a pause in her mopping and she smiled back, quickly washing her hands before leaving. The security man, fat with thinning black hair stuck to his greasy scalp, was too absorbed by his reality TV monitors to see her and she walked unnoticed back into a cold now joined by drizzling rain. She cursed a childish curse under her breath and pulled her hood up, making the most of any shelter as she walked back the way she came, past adult faces now a little brighter, steps a little lighter, all on their way home from the day's weariness to dinner, television and sleep.

Back home in the embrace of the bushes she struggled to remove her rucksack, eventually breaking it free and sitting it beside her before leaning back against the wall. Immediately she took the banana from her jacket pocket and peeled slowly, having learned to take her time with any distractions, savouring the feel as best her numbing fingers would allow before the first tiny bite, chewed over and over before swallowing, each time like a little life and death till the next, until eventually nothing was left but the skin. But then the skin became an octopus, then a spider, crawling up her leg, Mary's play terror building till it jumped onto her face. A silent scream. A silent giggle. Then it was a hat, stylish and practical, with built-in ear flaps. Perfect for this cold weather.

When her imagination had run dry she tore the skin into strips. Mary had learned toilet paper can take many forms and its need can be sudden. She lay the strips in a row to dry then unzipped her bag and gently lifted Carnation from the blanket, cradling her close such that their eyes met. Stroking her head she smiled, speaking quietly in a shivering whisper.

"I'm sorry, Carnation."

"What for, Mary?"

"Sorry I took you away from home. You're freezing. I can feel it even though you don't say anything. I should have left you warm in bed."

"I'm not sorry," replied Carnation. "Besides, they'd have thrown me out anyway."

"M..m..m..maybe not," stuttered Mary, teeth chattering in the early evening chill.

"Yes, they would. The second you were gone I'd be in the bin. That's the kind of people they were."

"You think so?"

"I know so. They didn't look after you very well, did they? So they weren't going to look after me," sneered the cat. "I'd remind them. Every day, every time they saw me. No, I'd be in the bin the second they'd given up looking. Or worse."

"Worse?"

"Yes, the incinerator."

Mary shivered but not from the cold this time.

"So maybe…maybe I saved you?"

"No maybe about it," purred Carnation. "You saved my life alright. Better a little cold than a whole lot burned."

Mary smiled and tickled Carnation tenderly behind the ear. "I'm glad you're here. I couldn't stand it otherwise."

"Till death do us part," the cat replied.

They sat quietly, veiled by the falling darkness as the traffic's rumbles faded and the voices stilled.

"Hungry?" asked Carnation.

Mary looked sadly into the eyes of her cat. "Starving, but it needs to get a bit darker. Then we'll go. Okay?"

"Okay."

CHAPTER 8

I looked at my watch then back at the mirror, and swore I'd burn all my clothes in the morning. In the space of forty minutes I'd gone from looking like a hobo to one of the Beach Boys and back again. It had become apparent that, other than going on holiday, I had bought no clothes whatsoever for about fifteen years. I looked at my watch again. Seven fifteen. Back to the mirror.

"Maybe they have a hot tub. Maybe I could just wear my Speedos? No, that wouldn't be weird at all, Tom," I muttered.

Another change and I looked again, turning one way then the other, but even without a tie the black suit still screamed 'Who died?'.

"Fuck it, my least old jeans and cleanest tee-shirt it'll be."

Five minutes later it was done, and they were ironed too.

"Who's the lucky lady?"

I looked at my watch again. Seven forty. Late enough to get the neighbours twitchy. Picking up the bottle of brandy, I considered bubble wrapping it in case I met with an expensive mishap on the way next door. But I decided it was a night for risks.

As I locked my front door I heard theirs open.

"There you are. I thought you weren't coming."

"I was just finding something to wear."

She looked me up and down but said nothing. She didn't have to.

Inside, Fred sat slumped in his chair with a smile as sincere as Donald Trump's, and an oratory to match.

"Alright, cunty bollocks?"

It was at that moment I decided I was going to fuck his wife.

"Stellar, Freddie. Absolutely stellar."

"It's Fred."

"That's what I said."

"You said, Freddie."

"Did I? Well, Fred, Freddie, what's the difference?"

"Freddie's like Freddie Starr. He ate a hamster. I've never ate a hamster in my fucking life."

"Never thought of that."

"Or Freddie Mercury? Maybe you think I'm a queer?!"

"Wouldn't dream of it. I'm sure your lovely wife doesn't either."

"What the fu-"

"Brandy, Fred?" I asked, brandishing the bottle.

He had two choices, both of which involved the bottle of brandy. He chose wisely.

"Yeah, go on. A large one," replied the pacified Fred.

I looked over to Samantha and nodded to the kitchen. "Can you show me where the glasses are?"

She smirked and led the way then, once inside, I turned her to face me. But a sudden nervousness took hold of her.

"Not yet," she whispered, before a kiss that was gone in an instant.

As she stretched up to get a glass my eyes took in the hard curve of her buttocks, the smoothness of her thighs, all generously revealed by her tight black skirt and I remembered the sounds through the wall. She turned and handed me a crystal glass, noticing my erection with a smile as she walked back into the room, me following behind, hiding nothing as I looked over to Fred, almost gone, just one large brandy from oblivion.

Samantha turned off the TV and sat back down, the room's silence suddenly broken by Fred's snoring.

"Doesn't it bother you?" I asked, smiling.

"It?" she replied, her voice irritated, suddenly defensive.

I nod at Fred.

"Oh, you mean *him*. My husband."

'*Fuck*,' I mutter to myself, sensing all was not yet plain sailing. "Yeah, Fred."

"Not Freddie?"

This has suddenly become confusingly hard work. I thought about taking my very expensive bottle of brandy home and salvaging what I could of the night. Maybe she sensed that.

"Sorry. It's…yes."

"Yes what?" I asked, having forgotten my own question.

28

"Yes, it bothers me." She looked over. "He wasn't always like that."

I went to speak, to ask the questions, but decided against it, maybe sensing the game was mine to lose and also sensing maybe I was a bit of a cunt. The answers came anyway.

"He used to be great. So funny. Ambitious too. He used to have his own company. Property development. Making a fortune."

"So…"

She took a drink and looked at Fred. "He met me."

I waited for her to continue but sensed I might have a long wait. "What do you mean?"

She said nothing for a while. I thought about asking again but then she spoke softly.

"It was great at first. With the money he had coming in we could do anything. Holidays to the Bahamas, Bali…We got married on St Kitts, had matching Bentleys. The business was booming, the future shone as far as life could see," she said, wistfully.

"So what happened?"

"Nothing."

"You've lost me."

"He needed an heir, or an heiress."

"Oh. Sorry. So you.."

"No. We had tests. He couldn't."

I look over at Fred, still snoring, now with added drool.

"That's a shame," I said, meaning it too. "He didn't take it too well, then?"

"It destroyed him. One day he was a king, the next, in his eyes, he wasn't even a man. I told him it didn't matter, I still loved him, but he'd made his mind up."

"So what happened then?"

"He just set out to destroy himself. Drinking. Drugs when he could afford them. He didn't care about the business so that started going down the pan, and his partners, well, they weren't the kind of people you let down."

"What do you mean?"

"They took everything. We had to run. Fred, he could barely crawl, but we got away." She looked around. "To this."

I saw the tears break through and sat beside her, wrapping my arm around her shoulder, feeling her tearful shudders and her hair soft against my cheek. So I took her upstairs.

Turns out I was the one being fucked.

Falling asleep in a married woman's bed when her husband was downstairs. Even a schoolboy wouldn't make that mistake. He'd be straight round to his mates, waving his still wet and shiny pecker like a badge of dishonour. I didn't even have much to drink. After we'd gotten 'it' out the way, twice, we talked for ages. Not what I was expecting. It just felt strangely comfortable. Too comfortable. I nearly had a heart attack when I opened my eyes to see 5:30 on the alarm clock. Samantha was snoring away, still curled up beside me. I looked around, half expecting to see Fred standing in the shadows with a murderous grin and a shotgun cocked and pointed. But the room was otherwise empty.

'So what now?' I wondered. 'Do I climb out the window, down the drain pipe? Maybe I should wake Samantha, at least say goodbye? Thanks?'

"Fuck it."

I got dressed and crept down stairs, wincing with every creak like a cowardly Ninja until the snoring switched from upstairs to downstairs. I let out a quiet sigh of relief as I saw Fred where we'd left him, then with something approaching pity I made my exit.

With the sound of the door softly closing, Fred slowly opened an eye, the second following quickly behind when the all clear was given. At first he didn't move, the weight of what he saw pinning him down, eroding whatever remained of him as he sat ruminating, first in self-loathing then in the more palatable anger. He pushed himself up from the chair before collapsing back into it, cursing as the numbness in his legs turned to pins and needles then fiery stabs in both knees. Gritting his teeth he waited for it to pass.

Eventually the treacherous limbs followed his commands without dissent and he stood, now wincing as the mutiny spread to his stomach. Quickly snatching a vase from the adjacent table he vomited the remnants of the previous night's excess which splashed against the glass walls. Somehow compelled to swirl the contents like a scientist with a beaker, he studied them, recognising nothing, another of life's little mysteries. He waited until the rebellion of his abused body abated then, still clammy-faced and sweating, headed for the kettle and the salvation of coffee and maybe, just maybe, toast.

Samantha awoke with a jolt, turning sharply to her left, finding relief at the empty space, smiling at the impression lingering in the mattress and the unkempt covers, a physical memory of the night before. She lay a moment, content to let the new day wait until she had finished with the night before, albeit more quietly than usual. She got dressed and went downstairs feeling something that felt like happiness before the imminent resumption of normal service. So she took her time washing out the cafetiere, grinding the Colombian beans and pouring first them then the water, waiting. Did he know, she wondered, surprised to realise that this time she didn't really care.

As she walked into the living room she saw him from the corner of her eye, sitting in his usual chair, with his usual mug, with the usual grey, lifeless look on his face. She closed her eyes briefly with a shake of the head when she noticed the vase.

"You always did exude class, Fred, though that looks more like some kind of casserole."

She sat down on the settee, turning her back on him and his tepid companion, and picked up the remote. Quickly scanning the channels, she settled on a repeat of *The Jeremy Kyle Show*. Living the dream.

"Maybe we should go on this, Fred. What do you think?"

Fred said nothing.

"Man leaves wife to run off with a vase of vomit. Bet even Jezza's never had that."

"What about woman fucks neighbour while husband sleeps downstairs."

"You mean while piss poor excuse for a husband lies downstairs in a drunken coma? Probably a bit run-of-the-mill for this."

"I'd never accuse you of being run-of-the-mill, darling," sneered Fred.

"I don't know how you can accuse me of anything, given the state you were in."

"You've never been the quietest."

"Well, it's been a long time since I've had anything to get worked up about that didn't need batteries."

"You fucking bitch." Fred made to get up.

"Sit down, Fred. We both know you're not going to do anything, don't we."

She watched as he slumped back in his chair. He looked back at her for a moment.

"We're in this together," he muttered.

Samantha stared at him coldly. "Remember that."

CHAPTER 9

As I sipped my second cup of coffee the jitters started again, slowly building into the cycle of guilt and dread and fear, old enemies I thought I'd long left behind. Hangovers had been a trigger in the past, but their strength seemed to have been worn down by my own stubborn stupidity, but maybe depression was more stubborn still, patiently playing the long game. I thought about having a hair of the dog but settled on just pouring the coffee down the sink.

My thoughts returned to last night, a night spent with another man's wife. As guilt squared up I fought back with the fact the other man was a prick. Yes, maybe I was breaking up a marriage, but it was a marriage that seemed broken beyond repair. Any lingering feelings she had for him seemed more the final glowing embers of pity than love. Besides, the sex was fucking amazing. But now what? An affair with all the cloak and dagger stress that comes with it? That was the last thing I needed right now. But…Fuck! Round and round we go.

Life had been empty since it all collapsed, severed into two neat pieces. Pre- and post-breakdown. But I had to go carefully, gently, and having an affair with the neighbour wasn't that. I did like her, though. My brain said 'friends'. My dick whispered 'benefits'. I gave up and left it to fate. It seemed less complicated that way. What a fucking idiot. But I did need to do something. The novelty of lounging around all day had become a bore, a gap that drink was only too happy to fill and DIY never would, merely a necessary evil, and with a new house there was no shortage of 'projects'. I still couldn't be arsed though.

But then I remembered Mary, and like the film said, there was something about Mary. I couldn't explain it. Maybe you could take the man out of social work but you couldn't take social work out of the man, as they say, or at least I did. For some strange reason I felt compelled to find out what had happened to her, even though it was almost certainly nothing. Was it to alleviate my growing boredom? Divert my random, spiralling thoughts away from self-destruction to something more philanthropic? I didn't really know. Probably both. But I had to do something. It was a choice between wallpaper and Mary…It was Mary.

The obvious first line of enquiry was to ask the neighbours, just not *those* neighbours. So I knocked on the door of number 54 with hope in short supply, expecting that within seconds the words, "Yes, they moved to Hull," would send me once more despairing to the Polycell and anaglypta.

As I stood there awaiting a response, I came to the conclusion that God hated me. That is the only explanation I could reach for him, or her, waiting till I'd knocked before opening the heavens. If I turned away now and they came to the door I would look like the oldest 'chap door runner' in town. If I stayed I was in genuine danger of drowning. So I stood there, trapped, eyes twitching between two front doors, head about to burst, then I heard a click.

It was a rather stern-looking old woman who answered the door to me. Five foot three with grey hair tied up, reflecting the good old days when buns were for women and samurai. She glowered for a moment as I stood in the pissing rain wondering how long it would take to scrape that last wall. Her steely grey eyes then squinted heavenwards, apparently sensing a biblical quality to the sudden flood.

"Are you a fucking Jehovah's Witness?"

I was a bit taken aback by the geriatric potty mouth. I was also about to be washed away.

"Do I look like a fucking Jehovah's Witness?"

"No. Unless you're undercover."

"I wish I was undercover," I replied, wringing out my sleeve for effect.

"Never heard a Witness say 'fuck' before. Guess you're not, so who are you?"

"I'm your new neighbour, can I come in?"

She looked me up and down. "You look a bit wet."

"No shi-"

"That's not colourfast, is it?"

Her bony little finger pointed at the blue dye running down my hand.

36

"You can't come in here if you're not colourfast. And that," she pointed at my tee-shirt, "would be the ruin of my new suite."

I stood, mouth open like a gawping trout.

"Why don't you go back home and get changed into something less destructive and I'll put the kettle on."

"Eh…Aye…Okay."

So I did.

I've never been a fan of Earl Grey but having no choice in the matter I sipped politely.

"You'll never be served that Tetley shite in here."

I smiled and raised my bone china cup, pinkie extended.

"The world's gone to Hell in a hand cart, son. But not here. Earl Grey. Loose leaf. No tea bags."

Bit harsh, I thought, blaming the decline of human civilisation on Tetley tea bags. But I let it slide, along with the revelation that I liked Tetley tea bags and she could get it right up her!

I settled on a conciliatory, "It has, eh." Thcn, fidgeting, "Sorry, in all the wetness I forgot to introduce myself. I'm Tom," I said, reaching out my hand.

She took it, rubbing with her thumb as she did. '*Christ, she's in the Masons,*' I thought, but as she studied her thumb I glanced down and noticed the residual dye on my hand.

"I scrubbed but I couldn't get it all out."

"Seems dry. You're not a sweater, are you?"

I thought of a sex joke but it didn't seem appropriate so I settled on, "No."

"Good. I'm Sylvia. I hate sweaters. Stink the place out."

I sniffed. "It does seem very fresh."

"My husband was a sweater. He had to go."

"Divorced?"

"No, Bridlington. Best place for him. The sea air helped to circulate it."

"Is he dead?"

"He might be. We didn't keep in touch after we lost Stan."

"Jesus, I'm sorry. Losing a child. I can't imagine."

"Stan was our dog until some bastard stole him. There was no way back after that."

I searched for a smile. Her face was stone.

"Oh. No kids?"

"Only Stan."

We sipped in solemn silence for a moment.

"And what about you?" she asked.

"Me?"

She looked around the otherwise unoccupied room. "Unless you see dead people? Do you have a family?"

"No, not even a dog," I replied, instantly regretting my flair for flippancy. "Eh, sorry. Must have been a difficult time."

After some excruciating silence I seemed to be forgiven.

"So, you're on your own then?"

"Yes."

"And what are you?"

"What am I?"

"What do you do?"

I prepared to give an indignant speech on how those were two very different things…Another time.

"I'm a social worker. Or rather, I was."

"Not enjoy it?"

"I loved it. Maybe too much."

"So what happened?"

I paused, looking at this little old lady stranger and thought about it, what happened, a question I'd never even answered to myself. But maybe a stranger was the only person I could open up to. Maybe it was time. So I did. I told her all of it, or at least all I could remember. All about the new graduate crackling with energy and the zeal and conceit of a prophet, desperate to solve all of society's ills at once. The early days, and it was no more than that, when I saw people as human beings, helped them, then went home and slept well, ready to help the next family in crisis. But the previous family in crisis hadn't gone away, the children you had helped now saw you as a liar and thanks turned to hate as they were taken away for their own good from parents to whom these children were now suddenly the most important thing in the world, and days of drink, drugs or just sitting on their arses were all over. Home to bed to lie for another sleepless night, might as well not go in, have a drink instead, might help me sleep, good idea, great idea. It's not a hangover, I'm just tired. Have a mint. Have a packet, but your breath still stinks worse than the person you're in to help, except they're not people. They used to be people, but that was before they became a case, then a case load, then an overwhelming case load, then the reason I couldn't eat, sleep, the reason I told my boss to go fuck himself, told HR I didn't need help and that they could stick their job up their arse, why kids weren't an option as they would be taken away, rescued from another drunken arsehole of a father who only a drunken arsehole of a woman would get pregnant with. I paused for breath, but before I could continue…

"So do I need to give you a slap or can you manage that yourself?"

"Sorry?"

"All that time spent wallowing in self-pity, blaming everyone else, expecting the world to solve all your problems. Maybe you don't have time to slap yourself. Maybe you're too busy, you know, with all the whining."

"That's not fair!"

"Christ, listen to yourself. You sound like a five-year-old. Well, if you were my five-year-old I'd kick your arse from here to Sunday."

"Well, I'm not, am I!"

Even I felt that was whiney. "Sorry."

"Look, Tom, if you're going to drink, drink. Enjoy it. And if you don't, stop."

"It's not that simple."

"It is. When Eric and I parted, well, I took to the sherry bottle for a while."

"No?"

"Yes. It started with trifles, just adding a splash at first. Then the splashes got bigger. Soon it was all splash and no trifle."

"No trifling matter," I couldn't help myself saying.

Her eyes hovered icily for a moment but then thawed as a smile appeared. "Indeed it is not."

"So what happened?"

"I got busy. I volunteered with the St Andrew's charity shop for a while."

"Good for you."

"It was a short while."

"What happened?"

"It was all church women."

"You not religious, Sylvia?"

"I told them they were talking shite. They asked me to leave."

"That'll be a no."

"I believe in God. I don't believe in shite. God must shake his head at the shite talked in his name."

"Amen to that. So what do you do with yourself?"

"I like taking pictures."

"Photography?"

"Is that what it's called? Christ, I had no idea."

She was a sarcastic old witch. I laughed and looked around, paying attention to the photos dotted all over the room for the first time. A few spectacular landscapes made all the more so by the rising or setting sun. I felt momentarily jealous knowing how many stunning sunsets I'd reduced to a coloured dot. But most of the photos were of people, unaware, candid and relaxed, lost in life's joys or troubles, a brief moment locked forever. In the early days of photography some people believed the camera took their soul. Sylvia seemed to have captured just that.

"I like photographing people best. I try and capture their soul."

She was also a fucking mind reader.

"You have a real talent."

"Everyone has a talent. You just have to find yours. Hopefully it's not moaning."

"I wouldn't know where to look."

Sylvia sighed. "You don't have to look, just find something to do to begin with. The rest will take care of itself."

"Well, now you mention it, that's the reason I came round."

"Oh? Not to show some manners to a new neighbour?"

"Eh…"

"Not just to turn my house blue?"

"Definitely not that."

"Well, that's something. So, spit it out."

"It's probably nothing."

"Which means it might be something."

"It's about…Look, she probably went to Hull or somewhere, after her parents split up…or just moved. I just got curious when I saw her name on my wall. Like I say-"

"Whose name?"

"Mary. Like I say, she prob-"

"She disappeared."

I leaned back in Sylvia's wingback armchair, sinking into it as her revelation sank into me. My eyes never left hers as my initial shock softened into surprise, then smugness. *'I knew it,'* I thought to myself. Next came shame as I realised I was feeling glad that a young girl had disappeared, reducing her plight to a chance for entertainment. I hid my smile behind a solemn face, but too late.

"You look like a dog with two dicks, son."

I sighed, then gave myself one of Sylvia's slaps, metaphorically speaking.

"What happened?" I asked, enthusiasm tempered, curiosity not.

"Good question."

I waited for a good answer. And waited.

"I take it the police got involved."

"Of course. A nine-year-old went missing, of course the police got involved," replied Sylvia, with no attempt to hide the irritation in her voice.

"Sorry."

"I'm sorry. She was lovely. Not like some of the other wee bastards that run wild about here. Never any trouble. Always a wee smile."

She drifted off somewhere for a moment, back in time. "When Eric and I…She was the only one that asked how I was. Not the grown-ups, only her. Nine years old, but an old soul. Then she

43

disappeared. We're supposed to protect them, aren't we?"

I saw her eyes moisten with sorrow and got up and sat beside her, holding her hand gently.

"Don't be getting my hand all blue now," she said, smiling as the tears ran.

We sat quietly but I knew there could be no retreat now. I had too many questions, and I suspected, a willing accomplice.

"When did she disappear?"

Sylvia didn't need to think. "Two years ago this month. She'll be eleven now."

"What happened to her parents?"

"They…It tore them apart. Especially when the rumours started."

"Rumours?"

"You know what people are like. Bloody gossips."

"They blamed the parents?"

"Not to their face. They were too cowardly for that. Just sad little people with nothing else to do. Maybe pointing at people from behind their curtains makes them feel important, I don't know. Makes my blood boil."

"I can tell. What about the police?"

"Bloody useless."

"No suspects? No theories?"

"They looked into the parents but found nothing, just two heartbroken people. Then it just seemed to peter out. A bloody disgrace it was. I think that's what finished Ann and Gordon. Ann left about a year ago. Gordon found it hard to

44

leave the house in case Mary came back, but in the end it was even harder to stay. He left six months later. It took a while to sell the house but…"

"Here I am."

"Here you are."

"So, what happened? I mean how did…Was she out playing or-"

"No. She just disappeared from home. She went to bed and then, in the morning, she was gone. Her bed had been slept in. The back door was wide open."

"Forced entry?"

"No."

"So did she just run away?"

"That's what the police thought after they'd checked out Ann and Gordon. They just put it down as a missing person. Passed the buck."

It seemed a reasonable conclusion to me too but I kept that to myself lest I receive a less then metaphorical slap. Sylvia was obviously convinced there was more to it than that, and being the newbie on the case I kept it shut. Or I thought I had.

"You think she ran away too, don't you."

I panicked.

"No! No! I…I have no idea. But you obviously don't."

"I don't know why I'm telling you this but, I ran away from home. I wasn't much older than her."

I looked at her in shock. "Why?"

She looked away. I'd gone too far.

"So I know an unhappy family when I see one. Ann and Gordon were good parents. Quiet. Kept themselves to themselves. But they loved their daughter. Never a raised voice. The walls in these houses are like paper so I would have heard. I can hear her at number 48 and that's two houses away."

I smiled.

"No, I would have heard. I would have known. It was something else. Somebody else."

We both sat back to think, to catch our breath. Although I felt Sylvia's sadness I knew I couldn't let it in, let it pull me down. As my mind settled down I looked around the room, a room filled with curios and character like the photos on the walls. One old man caught my eye, with a face like Sitting Bull, hair grey but thick enough to put my thinning barnet to shame. His eyes were bright with mischief. I wondered if he was still alive or if someone with eyes like those ever truly died. Then I saw her.

"That's Mary, isn't it?" I whispered, as if afraid I'd scare her off.

"Yes," Sylvia whispered back.

Over on the left was Mary on her way to school, back to the camera. I smiled at the size of her school bag, more of a rucksack really, imagining the weight of it filled with books. Then I noticed the little pink head of a cat sticking out of one of the pockets, a favourite toy. I could almost hear Sylvia calling out to her, see her head turn, her red hair ablaze in the sunlight, her embarrassment at

46

the sight of the camera as she stopped to please the grown-up.

But, as the button was pressed, her mouth smiled with a happiness her eyes didn't share.

CHAPTER 10

Even before her watch's battery had failed her, Mary had begun to time her life based on what was happening around her. Primarily the absence of things. The absence of people, of noise, of light: all brought safety and sometimes the chance to feed. So, in the quiet darkness, Mary found herself back at Tesco, but this time far from the main entrance. She sat for a time, hidden in the shadows watching but mainly listening, closing her eyes sometimes to heighten her hearing. No voices, no footsteps, only the occasional rumble of traffic safely in the distance, with the self-service fuel stop well out of sight.

Sensing she was alone, Mary emerged and crept towards the mesh fence surrounding the bins. She tugged at the padlock, which seemed far sturdier than the compound's contents merited. It was locked, so up she clambered as quietly as the mesh would allow, thankful for the absence of barbed wire. Safely on the other side she crawled in-between the bins, sitting, eyes closed and alert. Only when she was sure did she stand up. Only then did she realise the lid of the bin was too high for her tiny frame to reach. She silently cursed before looking around for something to stand on. A box. A pallet. But there was nothing. She sat back down between the bins to think, not ready to give up yet.

Then Mary smiled hopefully and stood up, lifting her foot against the side of the bin as high as she could and marking the spot with her left index finger. With her right hand she took out the lighter from her jacket pocket. She breathed in deeply then, flicking the lighter, she held the flame against the side of the bin and waited. She didn't have long to wait before the plastic began to smoulder and melt. Extending sideways as Mary moved the lighter, the hoped-for step formed before her eyes. When she thought it was big enough she drew back the lighter and waited for the bubbling to stop. Slowly she moved her fingers closer, sensing the heat before allowing them to touch, first in short taps then long enough to feel the plastic, warm but not hot and firm enough to stand on. Mary gently put her rucksack on the littered ground, mindful of her friend sleeping inside. She then lifted her foot to the newly created step and, leaning back against the adjacent bin for support, pushed upwards. Her heart rose with her as she opened the lid and gazed inside, her face beaming as food filled her eyes, as it would soon fill her stomach. For a moment she pondered the madness of all this waste, but only for a moment. She knew she must be quick.

Her stomach growled at the pictures of sumptuous hot dinners she could almost taste but knew she wouldn't, not tonight, maybe not ever.

Her thoughts drifted to a house with a kitchen, an oven, a table laid…But enough nonsense. She scanned for more practical choices and picked out sandwiches, fruit, crisps, bashed tins but with their ring pulls intact. Up and down she went until her rucksack was full and when it was she sat, allowing herself a brief moment of happiness as her glistening green eyes surveyed the bounty within, oblivious to the eyes watching from a distance. Satisfied, she climbed the fence with a new found zest, despite the load she now carried, and headed back through the shadows for home.

Cold, the curse of the homelessness, was now put to practical use as Mary's own refrigerator. She stacked the food in order of use by date and category, hidden by branches and leaves. Then, when content, she lifted Carnation and her blanket from the rucksack and sat them beside her before twisting the ring pull from the tin of spaghetti. Unzipping a pocket on the front of the rucksack, Mary took out a fork, dipped it into the tin and twisted, wrapping the contents round the fork with a splash. She felt the chill in her mouth and chewed, warming it as best she could before swallowing.

"One day we'll have warm spaghetti, Carnation," whispered Mary.

"Hot spaghetti," replied Carnation. "Cooked in a pot. You'll have to blow on it to cool it, it'll be so hot."

Mary chuckled. "We could cook it in a microwave."

"Better in a pot. And you could sit at a table, with your big plate of spaghetti."

"A huge plate of spaghetti, with steam coming off it. And chicken nuggets."

"And chicken nuggets, cooked in the oven."

"Not in the microwave?"

"No. Oven-cooked is better. Do you think I'd like chicken nuggets?" asked Carnation.

"I think so. You'd maybe want to pick off the batter. I don't think you'd like batter."

"I'll try it."

"Okay. And no cat food."

"I don't like cat food. I like Mary food," laughed Carnation.

"You're a very funny cat."

Carnation purred.

"I'm cold, Carnation."

"Me too."

"Do you really think we'll have somewhere warm again?"

"Yes."

"And hot spaghetti?"

"And chicken nuggets. But not until the bad people are gone."

"When, Carnation?"

"Soon, Mary. Very soon."

Mary sat content as she slurped her cold spaghetti, sauce splashing her. Finished, she drank the remnants of the sauce and wiped her chin.

"It's messy, isn't it?" smiled Carnation.

Mary's sauce-covered mouth spread into a grin. "It is. I think that's why I like it."

"You always were messy."

"They didn't like that, did they?"

"No, they didn't. Soon you can be as messy as you like."

"Promise?"

"Promise."

"Paw promise?"

Carnation held out her paw. Mary tickled it.

"Paw promise."

"I'm scared, Carnation."

"Don't be. I'll protect you."

CHAPTER 11

The next morning I awoke having barely slept, the hour or so's cat-nap I eventually got brought to a premature conclusion by Samantha saying hello to her little friend. I wondered whether it was for my benefit, a mating call of sorts, a desperate cry from someone seeking a new partner or a new life. But mostly I wondered about Mary. All night I saw those eyes, even in my brief dream, like a ghost who would haunt me until their story was known, justice served and they could finally rest in peace.

"Fuck's sake Tom, you've got her dead and buried," I muttered.

But even if she hadn't been taken, how long would a nine-year-old last on her own. I knew only too well how many grown men died every day sleeping rough, how many runaways got picked up by people offering a bed for the night, abuse briefly disguised as help. But she *would* be out there. As long as there was no body there was hope, to put it coldly, and if the police weren't going to look then I would. What the fuck else did I have to do? Coat the walls then re-coat them in a few year's time. Repeat until death. No, you wanted a purpose, Tommy boy, well here she is. Suddenly I felt responsible.

Where the fuck did I start? I could contact the police, who would tell me to piss off. I could pretend to be a journalist, freelance. But the cops would know all the paper guys. Then they'd tell me to fuck off. Or arrest me for identity theft, perverting the course of justice, wasting police time. Take your pick. I felt the sweat of anxiety.

"Why me?"

'Stop whining, bitch.'

Then I was in the kitchen, opening the fridge, glancing at the clock. It was precisely beer o'clock. I picked up a glass from the work top and poured in the Stella then noticed the milk residue float to the top and emptied it into the sink. Not much lost. I washed it out, filled it up, sat in the living room and drank my beer, then another, then another, waiting for my epiphany.

Ding dong.

But it wasn't Epiphany that had come calling, it was Samantha. I thought of her noises, looked at her tits and led her upstairs. Life suddenly seemed much simpler. But post coitus life was a different matter.

"We need to talk," said Samantha.

I sighed and lit a cigarette before offering her one.

"I gave it up. Never had to decorate since."

Duly noted, I thought to myself.

"We need to talk," she repeated.

"Fancy a drink?"

"Tom."

"Apparently we need to talk."

"Yes we do."

I sucked hard on the cigarette and held it, but I knew I'd have to let go eventually.

"Carry on then."

"Why are you being such a dick?"

"It's my super-power…Sorry. What do you want to talk about?"

"Us."

'Shit, there's an us?' I thought to myself. Out loud I kept it to just the last word.

"Us?"

"Yes, us."

'I thought you just liked sex. Fuck's sake, did you hear yourself earlier on?!'

"What about us?" I asked.

"Where are we going?"

"Why not stay right here. This is nice." I turned round to face her and smiled, my hand sliding up her leg. It didn't get very far.

"I'm not switching from one waster to another."

Bit harsh, I thought. I could kill for another beer though.

"I thought we really connected last time," she continued.

I'd always wondered if people really talked like that.

"We did, babe." *' Babe?! Get a fucking grip, Tom.'* "It was great. You were great."

"I meant the talking. I really opened up to you."

"The talking was great too. That was the best part." *'Don't push it, Tom.'*

"Really?" she asked.

"Yes, really. It was a great night." *'So why fucking spoil it with all this pish?'* "Look, I like you, Samantha. I really do. I like being with you but I don't want to risk spoiling things by rushing it…It means too much to risk." *'She'll never go for that.'*

"You mean it!?"

'Christ, she has.' "Of course."

I smiled as my hand met no further resistance.

Five minutes later.

"Fancy a drink now?"

"Might as well."

Downstairs I poured myself a beer and turned to Samantha.

"Beer?"

"Gin and tonic."

I looked up at the clock. Twelve-fifteen. "Bit early for the hard stuff."

Samantha's eyes screamed *'Go fuck yourself!'*

"A double," said her mouth.

"As the lady wishes."

"You sound just like Fred. A sarky, hypocritical little shit."

I handed her the drink as I stared coldly into her eyes.

"I seem to remember the other night that Fred was a good man who'd just lost his way. I seem to remember I couldn't say a bad word against him. I seem to remember you saying you still loved him. Not the words I would expect to hear from a lady who has her legs wrapped round the back of her neighbour's head. But it might explain my surprise at you throwing 'us' into the mix."

Samantha took a sip and sat down.

'You're sitting down? Isn't this the point where you storm out? Throw the fucking glass if you like but I've got more important things to think about than your fucking marriage dramas.'

She sat quietly for a while, making herself uncomfortably comfortable in my armchair while her mind processed all that had been said, filtering, twisting, looking for weaknesses to exploit as she lubricated the process of my demise with gin…My fucking gin. Sensing she was almost ready to rant I sucker-punched her.

"What do you know about Mary?"

Her face switched from indignant to bewildered, mouth hanging wide open, awaiting further information.

"Who?"

"Mary…" Then it dawned on me I didn't know her second name. "The little girl who used to live here."

"Mary McDonald?"

"Yes."

She took another drink, eyes studying me curiously. "What about her?"

"Well, she disappeared."

"And?"

"And?"

Another drink.

"She ran away. What else is there to say?" she shrugged.

"How do you know she ran away? How do you know she wasn't taken?"

She shrugged again, which was really fucking irritating. "I'm just telling you what the police said."

I got up and walked to the fridge. "What were they like? The family."

"I didn't really have much to do with them."

I smiled out of sight. *'Gordon, knock you back, did he?'*

"A quiet couple then?"

"Yeah. We invited them round a couple of times but…"

'But Ann put a stop to that.'

"Did you hear any rows?" I asked, sitting back down.

She shook her now empty glass at me, smiling. "Could you get me another?"

I seemed to be forgiven.

Handing her the drink I repeated the question. "So, did you hear any rows?"

"Now and then."

"What about?"

She sighed. "I feel bad saying this."

"What?"

"Mainly it was Gordon shouting at Mary."

"What about?"

"Just the usual stuff. Homework not done or her room wasn't tidy. Then she'd start crying. Then Ann would shout at Gordon. He could be a bit of a tyrant. Always a smile outdoors, though."

I took another drink feeling the effect start to kick in. Samantha continued.

"Like I say, I feel bad saying this. It must be terrible having your kids run away like that. Such a feeling of failure."

"And worry. I can't imagine."

"True. But then some of us don't even get the chance. Such a waste when you think about it."

"So you don't think there was any foul play."

"Foul play? Are you Hercule Poirot now?"

"Just curious."

"Why are you so interested?" she asked, glancing over her glass.

I told her about the marks and writing I'd found on the wall, but kept quiet about my talk with Sylvia for now. But as I started playing Hercule I didn't get far.

"So you've become fixated on a nine-year-old girl to avoid decorating your house?"

"Emm…"

I was about to point out she was eleven now but didn't see that helping so I got back to emming, then drinking, until eventually…

"There's more to it than that, " I whined.

"What? You don't have a job so you need something to do. Some purpose to get up in the morning?"

I searched for an argument but could find none.

Her eyes locked onto mine. "I understand boredom, Tom," she said with an ache in her voice. She took a long slow sip from her glass.

"But there are better distractions than chasing ghosts."

Was she right? Was it just a selfish distraction? I was suddenly unsure. Then I felt her foot between my legs and certainty returned with new purpose, at least until boredom, self-loathing and all their playmates returned, but now, along with them would come, Mary.

Actually Mary never left. Even when we were going at it, I was trying to figure out how to proceed with my investigation. It did feel more than a little creepy thinking about an eleven-year-old as we were grinding away but it did wonders for my staying power. Samantha seemed to sense something was amiss and upped a gear, drawing my full attention, or maybe Jeremy Kyle was about to start. But as our frantic pounding reached its sweaty climax we collapsed in a heap and I reached for a cigarette. Immediately I thought of decorating and cursed her for her subliminal destruction of this simple pleasure, but at least there seemed to be no further talk of 'us', and for that I was grateful. She may have been even more fucked up than I was and able to read two pages at the same time but she could certainly ding my dong and relationship-wise that would do for now.

CHAPTER 12

Samantha closed the door quietly behind her. Finding Fred conscious in the living room she headed for the kitchen and poured herself a drink before joining him.

"You've started early," said Fred. Eyes on the TV.

Samantha stared at his own glass. "We should get a bar installed in the living room. Cut down on all that unnecessary walking."

"I wasn't talking about drinking."

"Are we on that again?"

"Interesting choice of words, darling."

Fred put down his drink, got up and sat next to her. "It's not too late."

"What are you doing, Fred?" she asked as his hand rested on her shoulder.

"We're still…us, aren't we?"

'Christ, did he hear?' she wondered.

"What do you mean, us?"

"You know, like we used to be."

"We haven't been us since you stopped being you."

"I can get him back."

"I'd like to believe that, but I really can't see how."

As she twisted her shoulder away, Fred's hand fell onto the back of the couch, but his eyes were fixed on his wife.

"I know I fell apart after…Why don't we start again? We could adopt."

"Not going to happen, Fred."

"But think about it, our own child living here with us. It would be perfect.

"Perfect for you."

"Perfect for both of us. You want it too. I know you do."

"No, Fred. You always wanted it, I just went along with it. You were all I wanted."

"Well, go along with it again."

"No, Fred."

"Could anything be worse than how things are now?"

She stared at him. "We both know the answer to that."

"You'd be a good mum."

"Is that what you'd call it?"

Samantha got up and poured another drink, returning to sit in the armchair opposite her husband.

"Do you love him?" he asked.

"Who?"

"Him next door."

"Tom?"

"Yes. Tom," he sneered.

"Don't be stupid."

"So why?"

"Because he can get it up, for one thing."

"That would change too. You know it would."

"Yes, but what about me?"

"What? Would I get in the way of you fucking your precious Tom?"

"That's not what-"

"I don't know why you don't just move in?"

"Maybe I will. It would save money on batteries."

"Ha, he's just using you until he finds someone younger."

"He's not you, Fred."

"What's he up to anyway. Does he even work?"

"Like you, you mean?" she laughed. "He used to be a social worker."

"We're living next door to a kiddie snatcher?"

"Ex."

"Once a-"

"He was asking about Mary."

"Mary next door?"

"What other Mary? Queen of fucking Scots?"

"Why's he asking about her?"

"He found some marks on the wall when he was decorating."

"Marks?"

"Yes, the height thing. Mary McDonald aged…whatever."

"What else?"

"Nothing. He just wondered what happened to her. I told him she ran away."

They both sat and drank their drinks in silence.

"Just think about the adoption, eh?"

CHAPTER 13

After Samantha finally left, I had anticipated paint-blistering screaming to sear through the wall, quickly followed by St Tom saddling up his white stallion and charging through to save her and her collection of sex toys from the bottle-wielding, halitosis-breathing, Fred. But after ten minutes my imperious steed, Neddie, was tied up and munching oats, figuratively speaking, and I was thinking about beer. But only for a second, before I put the kettle on, poured a cup of Tetley and sat down to finally concentrate on Mary.

My first thought was to contact the police as they were the ones who had investigated the case. But why would they waste time talking to any old Tom, never mind Dick or Harry, about a case they had closed, though they would never admit that. Their response, I reckoned, would be instant defensiveness if even that. Maybe if I found more to go on I could speak to the police, but that was in the distance. I needed somewhere to start.

My second thought was the one I went with. Social work. There I was at least an ex-player. I knew how the system worked and I knew people to talk to. I sat nervously scrolling through names in my mental rolodex, flicking past the 'by the bookers', 'jobsworths' and 'career politicians', searching for potential allies, risk takers, friends or enemies with short memories, anyone who didn't think I was a complete cunt. I could only think of one name and even they might struggle with the last criteria. I searched my phone, smiled, dialled and hoped.

"I thought you were dead."

"Not hoped?"

"Now you mention it."

Emma's voice had lost none of its comic melancholy. Like Eeyore on a wet weekend in Grimsby. I sometimes wondered if she put it on, so disconnected was it from the childish twinkle in her eye. But if she did she was as thorough in her mischief as she was in her work.

"So…How are you?" she asked. "It's been a while."

"I'm okay. Can't complain."

"Still drinking?"

"Still direct as ever," I replied, my smile unseen. "I'm sitting here with a mug of tea and a Hobnob," I replied almost truthfully. Hobnobs seemed a more 'life is good, all is well' option compared to the 'one pay cheque from disaster' reality of the solitary rich tea quietly whimpering on the table.

"My favourite."

I made a note to buy some next time I was in Tesco in case proof or bribery was required. As I wondered whether chocolate Hobnobs were a step too far, Emma interrupted.

"I'm a bit busy, Tom, with work. I'm sure you remember…Sorry that came out wrong. What can

I do for you? I assume you want something…Again, sorry, that's not what I meant."

I thought about letting her go round like this for the rest of the afternoon, as I knew she could. But I hoped we would soon both be busy.

"I'm phoning about a girl."

"I may need more."

I pictured her sarcastic grin and knew I'd made the right choice.

"Mary McDonald, 52 Millar Street."

"What's the story, Tom?"

"She disappeared a couple of years ago. Officially she's a runaway but I'm not so sure."

"So what do you want from me?"

"Can you look and check if she's on the system anywhere?"

"Any reason she should be? The system isn't anymore joined up than when you were here so any pointers would help."

"I honestly have nothing, Emma. See if her name comes up anywhere. School, police, child protection. I know it's a big ask."

"I'll have a look."

"Thanks Emma."

"Can I ask, Tom, what is she to you?"

"Nothing really, just a name on a wall."

"Name on a wall?"

"I just think there's more to this case. I think the police have just…You know how it goes sometimes."

"Yes," she sighed. "If nothing else you always had good instincts."

"If nothing else?"

"Let's not," replied Emma, firmly. "Give me a couple of days and I'll call you. Don't get your hopes up though."

"Thanks, Emma. It's been good to speak to you again," I replied truthfully.

There was a pause. "You too, Tom. Speak soon. Bye."

"Bye, Emma."

I hung up, sipped my Tetley and dunked my rich tea.

"Fuck."

I should have listened to Peter Kaye.

Two hours later I found myself trawling Tesco for contingency Hobnobs (plain, who wants chocolatey tea), enthused with life for the first time since a previous existence, desperate to explore all avenues at once, just like the old me. The old me that had imploded.

'Learn your lesson, Tom Walker,' I muttered to myself. Yet I continued helplessly, impatient to feel whole again. I could only imagine what passing customers made of this gibbering madman, his face changing expression with every flickering thought, oblivious to being one alarmed phone call away from the very agencies I would need to convince of more than my sanity in the coming days.

It wasn't the words, "Are you okay?", that brought me to my senses, but the fear behind them.

"Sorry," I replied, my forced smile doing little to put the young mother at ease.

I decided to leave for home immediately, leaving the Hobnobs behind, and wait for Emma's call. I also decided that when it came I would be sober.

CHAPTER 14

At first the sniffing was far away, then closer, right up to her left ear, wet now as Mary drifted. It was the rustling which snapped her awake, tentative and curious at first, then knowing and frantic. Mary sat bolt upright turning to the noise as the black Labrador's snout drove into Mary's larder. Panic froze her as she watched the dog tear open a sandwich box, slobbering over the contents - contents which were to have been Mary's lunch. She clenched a fist and punched into the dog's side. Then again, harder this time. But again the dog didn't flinch, gorging on chicken and wholemeal bread. With tears in her eyes she looked around, picking up a stick, snapping the end into a point of sorts and rammed it into the dog's neck hard enough to cause pain but no damage. It yelped in shock, obviously unused to violence, turning confused to face its assailant. Mary stabbed again and the dog ran, bursting from the bushes towards its owner. It cowered, whimpering as the elderly lady tried to comfort her companion while struggling with her own shock and fear.

"Oh Henry, what happened? Are you alright, my darling?"

She looked over to the bushes. "What's in there? Did a bad dog bite you?" She examined him oblivious to the rain now falling, focused entirely on her beloved Henry. Finding no signs of injury, she patted his head and turned her eyes to the bush.

"What's in there?" she wondered aloud, stepping towards it.

"Can you spare any change, Mrs?"

The lady turned to face the voice, recoiling at the sight of the man, obviously a rough sleeper, standing far too close for comfort.

"Please. I'm really hungry. Just a little to buy something to eat."

She looked at him in disdain. "To eat, eh?"

"Yes. Please."

"Well, we all know what that means. Come on, Henry."

She walked off, Henry at her heels. "This used to be a nice park," she muttered. "I think we need to find somewhere else for walkies, Henry."

The man watched as they hurried to the exit, turning right and disappearing behind the wall. He then turned to the bush, watching for a moment before he too walked away.

It was a long time before Mary felt free to move. Free even to breathe. She turned to her supplies, relieved to see there was little harm done, before pulling her knees tight against her chin to feel warm, to feel small and hidden. After a while she opened her rucksack and lifted Carnation out, sitting her on her lap.

"I'm scared, Carnation."

"I know."

"Aren't you?"

"No, but that doesn't matter."

"I wish I was brave like you."

"You are."

"But I'm scared, how can you say I'm brave."

"Because you're alive."

Mary said nothing.

"Being scared doesn't mean you're not brave, Mary."

"I wish I wasn't scared though."

"Someday you won't be. Someday you'll be safe, you'll see."

"Are we safe now?"

"Why, did something happen?"

"A dog came in. It ate a sandwich."

"Not the chicken one?"

"Yes. Sorry, Carnation."

"It's not your fault, Mary. What did the dog do then?"

"I scared it away with this."

Mary held up the stick.

"That looks sharp."

"It is, and it ran away. But its owner was coming to look, but then a man spoke to her and…she seemed scared."

"Scared? Why?"

"I don't know. I think the man was poor. He asked the lady for money for food. That seemed to upset her. Maybe she was poor too and didn't have any money. Maybe that's why her dog was hungry."

"Then what happened?"

"Nothing. They all just walked away."

"Strange. Good, though."

"He was called Henry."

"The man?"

"The dog. I sort of liked him. But I had to stab him. She said they wouldn't be back."

"Well, that's good too."

"Do you think we're safe here?"

"As safe as anywhere for now."

"I'm glad. I don't want to move again. It's nice here. And it has a Tesco."

Carnation purred.

CHAPTER 15

And when the call came, sober I was. It was 3.15 p.m., two days later, when Emma's name came up on the screen, though strangely I'd known the caller's identity from the first buzz in my pocket.

"Have you found anything?"

"Hello, Tom. How are you? I'm fine, thanks for asking."

"Sorry, Emma. Hello, how are you?"

"Still fine, and yes, I have. Can I come over later? Six-thirty?"

"What is it?"

"Not a huge amount but we can discuss it later when I'm not doing the work thing."

"Okay, sorry. I keep forgetting. Thanks Emma."

"What's your address?"

"52 Millar Street."

"Isn't that…"

"Yes."

"I'll see you later, Tom. Bye."

"Bye."

It would be a long three hours.

I got up and went into the kitchen, past the half full bottle of Jack Daniels to the kettle, filled it up and switched it on. I waited. Then I got the teabag and the Trainspotting mug, opened the fridge, chose life and ignored the beer, all seventeen bottles of ice-cold Stella, took out the litre of semi-skimmed and waited some more. Click. Pour. Brew. Wait some more. Eventually I had tea. The first of many. I think I mentioned it would be a long three hours.

I had promised myself that I wouldn't do this; that I would wait for Emma with an open, calm mind. I break a lot of promises. By four-thirty everyone from MI5 to the Saudis were involved. And why was Sylvia so paranoid about Jehovah's Witnesses turning up at her door? Could they be involved too? I needed a drink. A drink was the last thing I needed. More tea. More caffeine. Eleven mugs of Tetley later I was a wreck. That's when the doorbell rang. I looked at the clock. Six-thirty.

"Thank fuck."

I opened it, and the door to my house became the door to my past as the familiar face stood before me. Christ knows what she was wearing, though it was more the 'why' that was the mystery. A banana-yellow dotted mini-dress with the dots growing in number at an alarming rate as the rain fell.

"Hi, Emma. Seasonally dressed I see. Come in, come in," I said.

'Before the dress shrinks any more, though you always did have nice legs'

I showed her into the living room, feeling suddenly anxious as she looked around.

"Nice."

Judgement passed, I relaxed.

74

"Tea or coffee?"

"Tea please, and I'll have one of your Hobnobs."

"Eh, I'm out of Hobnobs. Sorry. Rich tea?"

"Chocolate digestive?"

"No."

"Plain digestive?"

"No."

"Custard cream?"

"No. Only rich tea. Sorry."

"Rich tea's fine," came the unconvincing reply.

"Actually I'm out of rich tea."

I returned with her cup and another apology, sitting beside her as I tried to steady my mind rather than besiege her with questions. As she sipped I saw her eyes look down, realising my fingers were playing some manically random piano concerto, possibly in A minor, but as I don't play the piano that was a bit of a guess. Whatever key it was in I brought it to an abrupt halt. Not abrupt enough.

"Are you on something, Tom?"

"Tetley."

"How much."

"It might be eleven. Actually, this might be twelve."

"Twelve cups of tea?"

"Mugs."

"Christ." She smiled and shook her head.

"You know me."

"Did you ever try the meditation technique I showed you? I find it really helps calm you down."

"I tried it once, but my breathing was really fast so I tried slowing it down. Passed out. Woke up ten minutes later with a fucker of a sore head and a bump to match."

"Maybe some people are just naturally wired."

"That would be me."

She turned and crossed her legs towards me, dress rising further as I tried not to notice.

We both took a sip then got to it.

"So?"

"Mmm?"

"What did you find out?"

"Well, she is on the system."

"Why?"

"It was the school that brought it to us."

"Brought what?"

"That's where it gets a bit vague. Seems she had been a lively, happy girl since starting school. Bubbly was the word used. Always smiling. But then…"

"What?"

"She just stopped smiling. Her school work started going downhill too, but it was the change in mood that was noticed most."

"Changed how?"

"She became withdrawn."

"Not aggressive? Emotional?"

"No."

"Was she being bullied?"

"It seems not. The school say they looked into it."

"Yes, I'm sure they take bullying very seriously and they have a robust anti-bullying policy, blah blah blah. How many times have we heard that?"

"I know, but they obviously recognised something was wrong."

"Just nothing to do with them."

"Always the cynic."

"Comes with the job."

"It didn't have to."

"We can't all be St Emma…Sorry."

"I don't let the job get to me, Tom and I'm not going to apologise for that. I couldn't do it if I did."

"Look at me, you mean."

"You said it." She took another sip of her tea. "Why didn't you answer my calls?"

I felt myself quietly drift back.

"I couldn't talk to anyone. I was scared of my own shadow. Then when things became more manageable, I just got drunk. I was too embarrassed to talk to you or anyone else. Eventually it just seemed easier to ignore the past and start again."

"It hurt, Tom."

"I know. I was a coward."

"You weren't a coward. You were ill."

I felt myself squirm at the unwelcome scrutiny and the stirrings of a past that, while never dormant, I had at least managed to sedate.

"Sorry, Tom, I don't mean to bring it all back up. I've missed you, that's all."

"I've missed you too."

And I had. For a while I had thought that she might be the one until I turned her into the one who got away. I looked into the crystal blue softness of her eyes for a moment, feeling the warmth and the loss.

"Maybe we should get back to Mary."

She smiled, maybe recognising something of the old me. The good part, at least.

"So the school were convinced she wasn't being bullied, but knew something was wrong, something outside school, so they called us."

"Passing the buck?"

"We have to assume not, but it wasn't my case so I can't be sure."

I wriggled in my seat as I tried to contain the caffeine grenades I'd set off.

"Whose case was it?"

"Shirley Welsh."

"Who's she?"

"She started not long after you…left. She's young and pretty inexperienced, especially then."

"Did you talk to her?"

"If anyone knew I was discussing a case with you I'd get the sack. You do remember you're not a social worker anymore."

"Usually…Sometimes…No, not really."

"Do you ever think about coming back?"

I thought for a moment because the truth is I never had. Not for one fleeting moment in those two years, until now.

"We'll see how this pans out."

"You need to stay off the radar or we'll both be ex-social workers."

"I know."

"Seriously, Tom. I love my job."

"I remember that much. I promise."

"Good. So anyway, Shirley visited the family. They'd noticed a change in Mary and said they were planning on speaking to the school about it. Shirley explained the school had already been in touch, filled them in on that. Then she asked how things were at home."

"Then they got defensive."

"That's how it usually goes, but no. Shirley wrote that they seemed more concerned for Mary than themselves."

"Were they faking it?"

"Shirley thought not but, like I said, she was green and families can be good at hiding things."

"Then?"

"Nothing."

"No medical exam?"

"Monitoring."

"What did Mary say? She did talk to her?"

"No."

"Fuck's sake."

"I know. She was-"

"Green. I know, but even so. Fuck's sake."

It was Emma's turn to fidget.

"So did the *monitoring* show up anything?"

"She ran away a week later."

"You mean, disappeared."

"The police-"

"Assumed. But even if she did run away, did anyone find out why?"

"No. Not our area. It's…"

"Shite."

"Pretty much."

"Was there anything in the police investigation, if you could call it that?"

"Just that there was no sign of forced entry so…"

Caffeine-charged anger clawed at my insides.

"Any mileage in speaking to the police?" I asked.

"You can't, Tom. Neither of us can, remember that."

"What about Shirley?"

"What about her?"

"She could ask."

"You're not listening, Tom. No one can know we're looking at this."

"Okay, okay, I get it."

"Can I trust you, Tom?"

"Of course you can trust me."

I picked up the lukewarm mug but put it back before it got anywhere near my lips.

"So, where to now?"

"I don't know if there's much I can do other than-"

"Monitor?"

Emma shrugged. "If she appears it'll be flagged up on the system."

"And if she doesn't?"

"She'll stay missing. Maybe that's what she wants."

"No child wants to be all alone, God knows where."

"They do if they're scared enough. How many grown men do we see sleeping rough because, hellish as it is, it's better than the alternative, better than going home."

"They're not eleven!"

"I…"

"Sorry."

Emma stood up to leave.

"Please don't go. I'm sorry I shouted."

"It's okay, but there's nothing more I can tell you about her."

"Well, stay and tell me about you."

"Tom."

"We could talk about us."

"There hasn't been an *us* for a long time. Bye Tom."

I struggled to raise myself from the couch and walked her to the door, knowing there was no point in asking her to stay again, and knowing I needed more than pity. Maybe that was some kind of progress.

CHAPTER 16

An ache began to seep into Mary's joints,
spreading from her back and legs, out through her
knees and shoulders. She couldn't sit much longer.
She stretched her legs out as quietly as she could,
avoiding rustling leaves and breaking branches.
Turning to her makeshift larder she rummaged
around, picking out a big, red apple. She bit deep
and tore off a piece, chewing, the juice moistening
and freshening her mouth and tongue while the
skin and fibres cleaned her teeth. When all that
remained was a very bare core she opened a
sandwich. Roast beef. Not chicken, but still nice.
Finally, when she was full, an adjacent downwind
bush and some leaves took care of toileting.

Back in the living area, Mary unzipped one of
the rucksack's pockets and took out a notepad and
pencil. Inspecting its blunt tip she searched until
she found her small pocket knife and sharpened
the pencil to a long point. Then, as she did every
morning, she marked the day of the week, writing
'SA' for Saturday. She'd thought it was, but now
certain she smiled like every other child. Yes, there
was no school today, but for Mary it meant
something a little different. It meant she was free
to go outside free of suspicion. She smiled and
popped her things back in the rucksack, zipped it
and crawled to the edge. Then she listened. For

five minutes, maybe more, she listened for sounds of life, of danger, or stupid dogs or dirty men. When all seemed quiet she crept slowly out, pausing as her eyes adjusted to the light, scanning the park one last time before, in one seamless movement, she emerged upright, walking, just another child in a park.

Mary headed in the opposite direction to the previous day. The streets were noticeably quieter, pedestrians and drivers content to lie in bed or enjoy the morning with the TV or a book or playing with their children. Mary could almost hear the laughter before sadness dragged her back.

'Not for you,' it scolded.

Welcome as the weekends were they brought a different danger. Fewer people meant fewer customers to hide amongst, rendering shoplifting more hazardous. Her successful expedition to Tesco meant that there was no pressing need for food, but water never seemed to reach an expiry date and bottles never seemed to get bashed.

She entered a small grocery store, walking past the Asian man at the counter and feeling his eyes follow her as she drifted from item to item. She stood at the chilled section feeling anything but, trying to be invisible but feeling the scrutiny that all unaccompanied children encounter in such places. She picked up a bottle of water, studied it before exchanging it for another, flavoured, neither noticing nor caring which. Another exchange. Then another, hoping to wait him out, hoping the eyes she felt would move elsewhere, but…

"We do sell them, you know," said the shopkeeper sarcastically.

Mary sensed his suspicion wouldn't be shifting anytime soon. Her pulse quickened, eyes flickering to the door and back.

"Are you buying that or not?" he asked sternly.

Just at that a woman entered. "Sit, Henry. I'll be back in a moment."

"Ninety-nine pence? What a rip off," said Mary, returning the bottle and easing past the woman. Outside she recognised the dog, reaching out to pat it, but the dog recognised her too, pulling back and emitting a low, unforgiving growl.

"Yeah, well, get your own breakfast, fatty."

Curled up in her blanket, Carnation chuckled.

Mary turned away still thirsty, heading off in search of plan B.

As the wind whipped up, Mary lowered her head, tucking her chin in tight to shelter her face from the chill's teeth, watching the multi-coloured litter dance randomly about the street. A plastic bottle rolled into her path. Instinctively she pulled back her foot to launch it as far as she could, but just in time stamping down hard instead, stopping it dead. Now she just needed something to fill it.

Mary walked on, wondering more with each step why it was so difficult to find water in one of the wettest countries in the world. In her mind she conceived of ways to use it, constructing funnels to collect and direct the water into whatever containers she could scavenge. But that was for later. In the here and now she was still thirsty, so on she walked, the rain mocking her at every step as she tried to keep her face dry while her eyes scoured for puddles deep enough to fill from. Then, having soaked the ground and the girl, the rain ceased. Mary, wiping the wet from her face, looked up, cursed the bastard rain and kept walking.

For how long she didn't know but long enough to be in the midst of houses and gardens and children playing. She stopped, at once fearful and fascinated, watching the girl in the red dress, older than Mary, and the smaller boy bouncing on the trampoline, yelling.

"Weeeee…Weeee…"

Then another joined them, a girl, smaller still. The boy pulled her up and carefully eased her on, bouncing her softly as if afraid he'd break her. To Mary's left two girls on bikes approached at speed, braking hard before dropping them to the pavement and running to the trampoline. They sighed at the sight of the toddler, their excitement turning to impatience as they hopped from one foot to another.

"Can we get a shot?" asked the bigger of the two, her long blond curls hanging wet and limp against her face.

"Me! My go!" replied the toddler defiantly.

"She's just got on," explained the boy, as the toddler crouched down with a grimace before springing up as high as she could, her feet barely leaving the surface.

"Meeee!"

"She's boring," moaned the other interloper, a short, dark-haired girl whose clothes struggled to contain her. She took off her glasses and wiped them, her improved vision failing to improve her mood. "Come on, take hur oaf. Jist a few minutes. We need tae go soon anyway, we're goan to ur Grans."

The other girl looked at the boy. "Come on. Please, Brian."

"I don't know. What'd you think, Linda?"

"Please. Just a minute."

"We've got Gran's," repeated the dark haired girl.

Linda looked at them suspiciously. "Yes, you said, Ashley."

Linda looked at the toddler who looked back at the sister who held her world in her hands.

"No. If you need to go in a minute it's not worth the hassle."

"But-"

"She'll still be crying by the time you get to your Gran's. No," said Linda, her answer final. Then she saw Mary.

"Who's that?" she asked.

They all turned towards Mary, staring at the stranger on their street, silent for a moment, searching their memories.

"Dunno," replied Ashley, wiping her glasses again. "Looks like a Gypo."

They stared again. Mary took an involuntary step back then held her ground. She knew running would draw attention, but then she already had that. She took another step back, turned and walked away, deliberately slowing her pace. Behind her she heard voices.

"She's away now."

"Let's go see her, Beyonce."

"Ah can't be bothered. Just leave her."

"Come on. Shift it." Ashley picked up her bike and got on.

"Ashley!…Okay, ah'm comin."

Mary now heard the clatter of bikes, the turning of wheels, the panting of lungs till finally…

"Hoi, you. Stop!"

They were beside her now, Ashley to her right, Beyonce to her left. Mary kept walking straight ahead.

"You don't come fae roon here, dae yae? You're manky. Ur you a Gypo? She's a dirty wee Gypo, in't she, Beyonce?"

Still Mary walked.

"Can yae smell her?"

"Aye, she's mingin. No washed fur weeks, huv ye, Gypo."

Then another voice from behind, distant but closing.

"Leave her alone, the two of you."

"She's a Gypo, Linda. Smell her."

"Just fuckin leave her alone!"

Ashley turned her bike sharply, cutting into Mary's path. Mary jumped to the left to avoid her, sending Beyonce crashing to the pavement.

"Ya wee bastard!" she wailed.

Mary walked on, eyes wide, locked straight ahead.

"Serves you right," said Linda. "You should learn to mind your own business."

"Look at the state e' your bike. That wee Gypo's pure wrecked it."

"Let's fuckin get hur, Ashley."

That was Mary's trigger to run. Knowing she couldn't outrun a bike she turned off the road, up the first drive into the garden, over the fence, voices following behind.

"Come on, Beyonce! She's jumped oor intae Mr Browns."

"Ah'm comin'!"

"Leave the wee lassie," yelled Linda, but her voice was growing distant.

Mary ran, propelled by the sound of feet behind her, climbing fence after fence. Were they getting further behind?

"Ashley! Ma knees sair."

"Come oan! Yae need tae get hur back."

"Ah cannae. Ah need tae stoap."

"Fuck's sake, Beyonce."

"Sorry, Ashley."

"Ach, stoap greetin."

"It's sair."

"Sake."

"We'll get ur next time, eh?"

"You fuckin get ur next time."

"Don't be like that."

"Stop greetin, Beyonce. Yur an embarrassment."

"Ah cannae help it. It's saaiiir…"

As the voices faded, Mary sat wedged between a garden shed and adjacent fence, lungs fit to burst, a trapped animal ready to punch, bite, scratch, tear…But the enemy didn't appear. But still she hid, eyes never leaving the gap, the only way in, or out.

There she sat until the light faded and the darkness fell. In the silence that came with it she finally crept back out into the world, scouring for danger in every direction bar one. Downwards. And that was how she fell, down to earth with a grunt and a grimace, holding any further noise inside. Getting to her knees she looked back, now seeing the garden hose that lay uncoiled like a snake ready to devour its prey. Mary smiled. Then she turned on the tap.

With her bottle filled she made her way to the end of the mono-blocked driveway, ritually looking left and right, hoping Ashley and Beyonce were with their Gran, that their Gran lived far away and that she had a violent temper and hated those wee bastards. Either way the street was deserted. Ready to move out, she hesitated, and with hesitation came realisation… She was lost.

Fear filled her, threatening to suffocate her if she stood waiting any longer. Before it could Mary just chose a direction and walked, desperately searching for the familiar, her pace quickening as her fear grew, breaking into a run as it became full blown panic. Caution was the next casualty, tossed aside as she ran the streets only to stop at every corner, desperate for recognition, overwhelmed by choices she was unable to make. Streets, roads and avenues, all with names that meant nothing. So she stayed on a straight path hoping it would lead her home eventually, ignoring the curious eyes and the concerned voices and their lies.

Eventually, cold, exhausted and still lost, Mary approached what appeared to be an abandoned church, boarded up against the elements. She froze momentarily as car headlights seemed to pick her out like an escaping POW before it passed her without slowing. She breathed out then jumped onto and over the low boundary wall, wincing at the sudden noise of gravel beneath her feet, each foot step bringing a running commentary of her movements.

Abandoned churches and vandals go hand in hand, and Mary was glad to see the hard work had already been done for her, allowing a quick entrance and shelter from the returning rain. Inside it was a similar story, with the church's booming echo amplifying her every step and each accidental trip over obstacles hidden in the darkness. As her eyes adjusted to the dim light leaking in from the streetlights outside, she was glad to see that the pews remained intact. Quickly settling on one, Mary unzipped her rucksack as quietly as she could and lifted out Carnation, blanket and all, resting her on her stomach as she scrunched the bag into a pillow and stretched out along the pew.

Carnation and Mary lay quietly, content to say nothing until Mary's stomach rumbled and she remembered the food.

"We've lost it all, Carnation," she wept.

"What?"

"All that food. Enough not to be hungry, not for ages."

"Ah. I am a bit hungry."

"I'm sorry."

"What for?"

"I'm sorry you're hungry because of me, because I got lost, because…"

"Don't be silly."

"But…but…" The sobs overcame her.

"We needed water too. Even more than food."

"We could be eating right now. Spaghetti. We had tins and tins. And sandwiches and bananas."

"We'll find it."

"But how? I've never been so lost."

"Then we'll find more food. I'm sure of it."

"Are you, Carnation?"

"Yes. Maybe even Sainsbury's. Or Marks and Spencer."

"Really? Maybe you're right."

"I know I am. Trust me."

"I do."

"And only me."

"Only you."

Mary's stomach growled. "I'm really hungry."

"I know. You'll have spaghetti soon."

"Warm spaghetti."

"Hot."

"Promise."

"Some day soon. Paw promise."

Then the silence took her. Then the stillness. Then the sleep. Deep, filling and delicious.

Mary awoke, gently stretching, eyes cracking open slowly, easing her into the soft light of a new morning. As she sat up she heard a rumbling sound from the other side of the church, tensing as she recognised it as snoring. Now fully awake and alert she quietly bundled Carnation into the rucksack and began to ease herself onto her feet. Suddenly she felt a hand on her shoulder.

"I was wondering when you were going to wake up."

Mary froze.

"Thought I was going to have to give you a little nudge, like. Thought you were dead at one point….Don't talk much do you? That's alright. Seen and not heard. No truer words."

He moved his hand from her shoulder slowly turning it around, the back of his finger tips now softly stroking Mary's cheek.

"You're a pretty little thing, even with the dirt. Been a while since you had a bath, eh? Not to worry, my lovely. I know a place, down by the river. Get you scrubbed up clean as a whistle."

Mary remained motionless as his fingers stroked her hair, his hand moving around, pulling her head against his shoulder, the stink of his breath filling her.

"It's not safe for a little girl to be all on her own. I could help you. Keep you safe. We could help each other."

As he slid his hand lower, Mary's body began to shake uncontrollably.

"You must be freezing. Come here, I'll get you warmed up."

A sickening crack silenced him and he slumped forward falling at Mary's feet with a thud. She didn't look down. Neither did she turn her head as a second man's voice spoke just behind her.

"Ah won't ask ye tae trust me. Monsters live in plain sight and that's where the danger lies. But ah think ye already know that."

He paused for a moment looking for comprehension, sensing only fear.

"Go oot the door. Turn left. Walk straight fur aboot half a mile. Turn right into Blackside Place. Now repeat whit ah just said."

Mary remained silent.

"Repeat efter me. Turn left…Turn left…Ye' need tae dae this…Turn left."

"Turn left."

"Walk straight fur half a mile…Walk st-"

"Walk straight."

"Fur half a mile."

"For half a mile."

"Turn right."

"Turn right."

"Intae Blackside Place…Intae Blackside Place."

"Into Blackside Place."

"Wance mair. Turn left."

"Turn left."

"Walk half a mile."

"Turn right into Blackside Place."

"Good girl. Now go."

Mary got up and turned to pick up her rucksack. As she did she glanced back at the man, their eyes meeting only briefly before she turned away. She looked down at the body at her feet. Maybe alive, maybe dead.

The second man spoke. "I'll take care ae him."

Stepping on the first man's head as she went, Mary made her way towards the door without looking back a second time. Out in the sunlight she paused, letting her eyes and mind adjust. Then she turned left.

On she walked as instructed and as slowly as her racing heart would allow, thankful for the lack of passers-by, the absence of rain and the sign up ahead.

"Turn right into Blackside Place," she whispered before crossing the road between a Vauxhall Corsa and a white van man. Then Mary turned right and kept going, past 'Ali & Son's' and 'Bet Fred', past 'Susie's Nails' and a 'Saint Andrews Hospice' shop.

"Follow the yellow brick road. Follow the yellow brick road," she sang without realising.

And she did. All the way to Tesco.

But Tesco could wait. As soon as she realised that she was no longer lost joy raised her up and carried her home, just another happy child playing in the remains of the weekend.

But as she approached the park, Mary slowed, her defences once more cautious and alert. She grew nervous at the sight of other children playing, wincing with each thud of a ball, each bell ring from a passing bike.

"Hiya. Watcha doin?"

Mary span round with a start and saw a blonde girl about the same size and age looking at her. But now, with Ashley and Beyonce's mocking voices ringing in her ear, she saw more. She saw how clean the girl was, and therefore how dirty she was, tensing at the memory of the previous day.

"Watcha doin?" the girl repeated.

"Nothin."

"Where you goin?"

"Nowhere."

"Must be goin somewhere."

"No. Just…going to sit here."

Mary walked to the park bench and sat down. The girl followed.

"My name's April, what's yours?"

Every question was like a dog gnawing on her bones.

"Agnes," she replied.

"Agnes? That's like a grannies name."

Mary said nothing.

"You're very dirty."

Mary sighed and wondered what a Gypo was.

"You smell too."

Mary decided to punch her in the face.

"April! Come on, we need to go. Dad's waiting in the car."

April stared for a second, oblivious to Mary's clenched fists and gritted teeth, but not her eyes. She stood up cautiously, walking backwards towards her mum who was struggling to hold on to a toddler with one hand and a terrier with the other. When she felt out of range she turned and walked towards her mother with an exaggerated swagger.

"Come on, hurry. Who was that?" asked her mother.

April looked back at Mary, smirking. "Just some wee Gypo."

"That's not nice," her mother replied, looking back, coming to the same conclusion.

It seemed to take forever for the park to empty but eventually it did, if only long enough for Mary to crawl back into the bushes, her bushes, her food. She sat and ate quietly as the sounds of people and their danger came and went, safe in her trap for now. She studied the leaves on the bush before tugging one free for further investigation, marvelling at the intricate structure. Moving it back and forth Mary positioned it beneath a ray of sunlight that had found its way through, examining its sinews and veins through the almost transparent skin, holding it beside her own hand for comparison. She stroked it between her thumb and middle finger almost apologetically, wishing she could put it back. She wondered what the bush was called and remembered school and a day out 'Nature watching', returning home with new dreams of being a scientist, but keeping them to herself, too afraid of being mocked as a swot. She studied the leaves around her, on the ground and on the untamed branches above, trembling at what lived beyond, wishing she was a tree.

She woke up not quite sure how long she'd been asleep. It was still light and noisy outside. She reached into her rucksack and helped Carnation out, softly rubbing and stretching her legs, scrunching her paws which she felt must be stiff and sore.

"Sorry you've been in there so long. I fell asleep," whispered Mary.

"It's okay. I fell asleep too."

"Are you hungry?"

"No."

"We need to keep quiet for a while yet."

"I know. Let's just lie here."

"Okay. I think it'll be dark soon."

"I think so too."

Mary's fear dissolved slowly with the darkness and the silence that came with it. She giggled as her stomach growled.

"I'm definitely hungry now."

Carnation nodded. "That *was* a big noise."

Mary looked amongst the fresh food, knowing it has to be eaten first before it went off. But then she saw a tin of macaroni and her stomach growled again.

"It's okay," purred Carnation.

"Are you sure?"

"Yes. The fruit looks nice and fresh. It'll be okay for a few days yet. Have the macaroni."

Mary tugged on the ring pull, her mouth watering as the contents were revealed. Her rapture was interrupted by another growl of her stomach and after a brief frantic search for her fork she savoured her first mouthful, chewing every piece over and over lest even a morsel of flavour be missed.

Carnation looked up into Mary's eyes. "Good?"

"Mmmmm," was all Mary could offer.

When every piece was gone and her tongue had licked as much as it could reach, she tossed the can into the refuse area of her encampment, feeling a little ungrateful as she did. However, her guilt was short-lived and she sat back against the wall, cradling Carnation in her lap. Wiping her mouth she looked at the sauce on the back of her hand. She rubbed it with her fingers, for the first time noticing the dirt as it was washed away by the sauce. She kept rubbing, spreading out across her hand till the sauce was used up, leaving only its stickiness. She stopped and said nothing.

"What's the matter?" asked Carnation after a while.

"Nothing."

"Okay."

"Carnation?"

"Yes."

"What's a Gypo?"

"I don't know."

"Is it someone who's dirty?"

"Maybe. I think so."

Mary studied her hand. Then the other. "I'm dirty, aren't I?"

Carnation paused warily. "Maybe just a little."

Mary's nose twitched as she sniffed the air around her, gradually bringing it closer to her arm pits. "I do stink a bit."

"My nose doesn't work very well."

"I think I do. Two girls have said so. Why else would they if I didn't?"

"Why would anyone be cruel? But we know people are, don't we?"

"Yes."

They sat and listened to a plane fly overhead, its flickering lights flickering even more so as it passed between the leaves. Mary thought of the people flying to the sun. Maybe to Spain to play in swimming pools as she had once.

"I don't want to be dirty."

"I know, but where will you wash?"

"I can wash in the pond now everyone has gone home."

"It'll be very cold."

"I don't care."

"You don't have soap."

"Do I need soap?"

"I think it would make you cleaner."

Mary sighed.

"Don't worry, I know where we can get some. But you'll need to wait till tomorrow. Do you mind being dirty for one more day?"

"Okay, one more day."

"That's all."

" Paw promise?"

"Paw promise."

"Then I won't be a Gypo anymore."

"Not a dirty one. I think I'd like Gypos."

"Me too. Bet they're not even dirty. Bet those girls are just bitches."

"Mary!"

"Sorry… Bet they are though."

Carnation purred as quietly as she could.

CHAPTER 17

Progress with Mary proved elusive and began with a lie, if a broken promise can be called a lie.

My first dilemma was on the scale of the lie. A big lie, while being potentially more effective, was also more likely to be scrutinised and therefore to end with my pants ablaze. A small lie was more likely to slip under the radar, but also more likely to prove fruitless. I can't remember who said *'if you're going to lie make it a big lie'*, but whoever it was I decided to take their advice. Thinking about it, it may have been the Nazis and they *were* the experts. I just hoped I didn't end up chewing a cyanide capsule in a Glasgow bunker when this was all over.

It was surprisingly easy to get my hands on props for the lie. A few clicks on vimtoprint.com and a couple of days later I was no longer Tom Walker, burned out ex-social worker. I was now:

Joseph Mason
Senior Reporter (Social Affairs)
Guardian Media

I had considered using my own name but baulked at the idea of a simple phone call and the words *'Never heard of him'* bringing my lie crashing down. For better or for worse, the idea of going to jail for identity theft never entered my mind. But any roving reporter needs to know who to rove to.

I knew the answer lay in the file Emma had, but also knew I couldn't ask without raising the obvious suspicion that I was up to no good and a lying bastard. I kicked myself for not photographing the file when Emma went to the bathroom, but then remembered she hadn't. I thought about popping in to the office on a social visit, pretending to catch up, but too much time had passed. I even thought about breaking in, but then I thought of Watergate, and with me not being the President of the United States of America, I'd be going to jail. I did a lot of thinking. Then I remembered Sylvia.

She seemed surprised to see me. Pleasantly, I think. She did smile when she said, "Oh, it's you." She also offered a cup of tea. Though I'd consciously reduced my caffeine intake since Emma's visit it seemed impolite to refuse. I also thought tea might bring biscuits, Hobnobs even. It didn't.

"So what brings you round as we've established you're not the neighbourly type?"

"Depends on the neighbour."

She stopped pouring.

I forced a nervous smile. "And the tea."

The pouring continued.

"I knew I'd civilise you."

I watched her watching me as I drank, checking I was indeed embracing the Earl Grey experience. My conversion seemed to pass muster.

"Lovely," I slurped, which seemed to violate some code eliciting a tut of disapproval. I still had a lot to learn on the etiquette front.

"So, other than neighbourliness and Earl Grey, what brings you round?"

I breathed in.

"Other than both of those things, I've been thinking about Mary."

"What about her?"

"I think you're right. I think there's more to it."

Sylvia seemed suddenly energised.

"Why?"

"Just my gut. And that photo."

I turned my head, shivering as Mary looked straight at me, straight through me, at something hidden from everyone else.

As we sat drinking our tea I told her everything I'd learned, my talk with Samantha, with Emma, the risks and my plan.

"You're a fucking idiot."

Not the ringing endorsement I'd hoped for, if I was being honest. I tried sketching in a bit of detail but that just upgraded me to an imbecile. Giving up any hope of encouragement I cut to the chase.

"You said you spoke to the police. Can you remember their names?"

Sylvia stared at me like a mother stares at an infant son who's missed the potty for the third time. She shook her head and left the room. I waited in limbo.

Having decided she wasn't coming back, at least not until I'd left, I went to get up. But return she did, holding her hand out towards me.

"He left this."

I took the card and looked at it. DS Simon Black.

"If you insist on this folly, start with him, but don't expect me to visit you in jail listening to you whine about being buggered in the shower."

I tried to reassure her that my sphincter had been well trained to prevent such an occurrence. She countered with afternoons drinking stewed Tetley tea. I had nothing. We sat quietly for a while until Sylvia broke the silence.

"I'm glad you haven't given up."

Back home, holding his card between thumb and index finger, I considered how best to approach DS Black, or should it be the less formal Simon. No, definitely the former. Cops didn't do informal. He probably made his mum call him DS Black.

I opened up the fridge and took out the bottle of orange juice that sat next to the beer. I looked at the beer, counted the bottles, checked the best before date of the orange juice, sighed and poured it into a tall glass, the kind you would use for JD and coke. Jack would know what to do.

I looked out the kitchen window watching the gale at play, bending branches, young leaves struggling to hold on, litter swirling in the vortex, knowing how it felt. In the back corner of the garden the neighbourhood feral cat sat, not on the mat, but on the rotting stump of a butchered conifer, as still as Buddha in the midst of chaos and decay. He looked up at me then licked his grotesquely oversized balls, just because he could. Or maybe it was a sign that it was time to find my own.

I rang the number and was surprised to be put straight through. Initially unnerved at the sudden reality of it all I decided to play it straight, apart from all the lying, and see where that took me. I was even more surprised that it took me to a meeting the next day at Alice's Café at one. Lunch was apparently on me. Then he hung up.

He'd seemed a bit taken aback at first, defensive even, but he'd relaxed as the conversation went on, seeming relieved. I was relieved myself that I hadn't needed to go down the implied threats and accusations route, knowing where that could lead. I'm sure Sylvia would be relieved too having, I'm sure, believed none of my sphincter bluster. I thought of a celebration drink, put the kettle on and lit a cigarette feeling oddly calm.

The next morning, actually I'd consider it more the middle of the night; anyway, I woke up at 5.36 a.m..

"Christ," I muttered, squinting at the clock in the hope that I'd misread it. Sometimes I wake up and look at the clock thinking only of the hours I have left to sleep. This wasn't one of those. This was a fidgety, ceiling-staring fucker from which there was only one escape. I got up. It was a morning for coffee, strong with a splash of milk. Only psychopaths drink black coffee, and maybe fictional private detectives, who were also invariably psychopaths. I took my coffee and my body and sat in my favourite chair to wait for my brain to work. That happened at about eight, my usual wake-up time. Minds can be stubborn but he'd made his point, freeing me to mull over how to play my meeting with the DS.

Come twelve I'd succeeded only in adding anxiety to my ignorance, having no idea what the uniform of a journalist comprised. How they spoke. Their jargon. I decided I'd go for the undercover renegade journo, blending in with society, outside the stiff conventions of Fleet Street.

'Maybe he knows everyone in Fleet Street? Where the fuck is Fleet Street?' I wondered.

I thought of cancelling or postponing the meeting to give me time to do some basic research. I thought of beer. I thought of Mary. I thought of Sylvia, her hope now rekindled by my own stupidity. I thought of Tetley, and wondered if they served Earl Grey in prison or whether even asking for it would be enough to lead to soap lubricated unpleasantness in the communal showers. Eventually I stopped thinking.

I arrived early, sitting near the back with a mug of tea for company through the waiting and the sweating, glad that Sylvia wasn't here to see it. He arrived dead on time and I recognised him immediately, even though I'd never seen him. You can always spot a cop. He seemed to recognise me too. I hoped the same was true for journalists. He nodded. I nodded back, my hand offering the seat opposite. As he sat the waitress was on us in an instant. She was beautiful. Lovely little black uniform…Anyway.

"Ready to order?"

"Can you give us-"

"Burger and chips, Coffee...black."

'*Christ,*' I thought.

The waitress turned her attention to me, and for a second I fell in love but she was only interested in one thing.

"And you?" she asked, lips sliding as she chewed her gum.

"The same," I replied, ready to match him.

As she left we studied one another. He looked mid-thirties, medium height with a muscular build. His hair was short and black with flecks of grey, framing a face showing the first signs of wrinkles. He had a scar on his chin that I sensed was a source of pride, and blue eyes that radiated a practised warmth but which I knew could turn cold in the proverbial New York minute. I watched as he gave me a similar once-over, him being a cop and all, and imagined what he'd see. I was to find out quickly.

I rummaged in my pocket and pulled out one of my shiny new cards and offered it to him. He took it, studying it with professional politeness. He sat it on the table looking at me with that same smile.

"You're no more a journalist than I'm Stephen Hawking's stunt double."

Fifteen quid down the drain. I thought of protesting but knew it would be pointless. Besides he had agreed to meet me, something Stephen Hawking never would. The waitress arrived just in time emptying her tray with practised ease and natural indifference. As DS Black sipped his namesake I yelled after her, "Excuse me. Sorry, can I have a splash of milk." The game was, after all, well and truly up.

The mouth said, "No problem," but the eyes don't lie.

"So who are you and what's your interest in Mary McDonald?"

As my milk appeared, I poured it, took a gulp and told him the truth.

"So, other than moving into her old house you have no connection with Mary McDonald whatsoever?"

He was a cop alright.

"Pretty much. But what does that matter?"

"I'm just trying to figure out why you're so interested. At the moment it seems to be a case of an unemployed man who's bored and looking for something to do."

I was hearing that a lot.

"I wouldn't argue, but again, what does it matter?"

"It matters because I have better things to invest my time in than keeping you entertained between game shows."

"Whatever this is, it's not that."

"Then what is it? Because even speaking to you about a case puts me at risk."

"It's…It's what made me want to be a social worker in the first place. Giving a fuck. Especially kids. Protecting them. Helping them build their lives. Keeping them safe, and Mary McDonald isn't safe. I feel it in my gut. I have nothing more to go on than that. Just my instinct, and it was usually, no, it was *always* right."

"So why did you quit?"

"I didn't quit."

"You're an ex-social worker. If you cared so much…"

"I'm an ex social worker because I cared so fucking much!"

I stopped, aware of heads turning towards us. He took another sip and looked me over once more, a little more forthcoming this time.

"Maybe you're not the Family Fortunes type."

"I know the protocols. I know the system and I know when to keep my mouth shut. All I want from you is what you know, and what you feel. Cops have instincts too."

He said nothing for what seemed an age. I thought I'd blown it.

"Officially it's a missing persons case. There was no real evidence of any crime, so the decision was taken to pass it on."

"Not your decision?"

"No."

"I get the feeling it's not a decision you agree with."

He shrugged.

"Then why?" I asked.

"Resources. Simple as that."

"Even with a missing child?"

"This is the age of austerity, don't you know, which I believe is Latin for fuck them."

I shook my head.

"So they put it down as a missing person, but what did *you* think?"

"I don't think it's a simple runaway story, if there is such a thing. There's more to it, but…"

"You think she was abducted?"

"I'm not saying that. Maybe. Or maybe she did run away, but not because she got told off for not doing her homework."

I was starting to feel we were going round in hazy circles as vague innuendos were tentatively tossed into the ring by a man uncertain whether he could trust me.

"I need more than that, and you want to tell me more or else you wouldn't be here."

"How do I know I can trust you? You've already lied about being a reporter."

"Maybe you can trust me because I'm not a reporter."

He smiled at that.

"Okay. I honestly don't know whether she was abducted or just ran off, we didn't get that far."

"But…"

"We interviewed the parents. They were in pieces. In my job you get a feel for whether people are lying."

He glanced down at my card, smiled at me, then continued.

"No one is that good an actor. They had noticed a change in Mary. They were going to speak to the school but then she disappeared."

"Did you interview her teacher?"

"I spoke to the headmistress and the teacher. I also spoke to a couple of pupils who knew her, on the fly, which was a bit naughty but, anyway, there seemed to be nothing that had happened at school to cause the change in Mary."

"And the parents?"

"They seemed nice people."

"They seemed nice people, so that was that?"

"No that wasn't fucking that."

His eyes burned a hole in me.

"It's not just you social workers, or ex fucking social workers, that give a fuck you know."

"Sorry, I…Sorry. So what happened then? Was that when you were taken off the case?"

"No."

His eyes locked onto mine again, no rage in them this time.

"And this is why I agreed to meet you."

He picked up his mug and drained the lukewarm remnants.

"How well do you know your neighbours?"

"Which ones?"

"The Turners."

"Who?"

"Fred and Samantha Turner."

"Ah. Not well enough to know their last name."

"Have you spoken to them?"

"Yeah, sure. A bit. They invited me round one night for a drink."

"And how did they seem?"

"Fine. They were…a bit fucked up, actually."

"In what way?"

"Just…Not getting on. Arguing. Sniping at each other. Typical married life, not that I'd know."

"A bit tense, would you say?"

"Yeah, probably. Why? Where's this going?" I asked

"Are you friends with them?"

"No. I barely know them. Like I said, I didn't even know their last name. What's this about?"

He paused a moment.

"You didn't get this from me. Remember that."

"Okay."

"When I was investigating Mary's case I checked the system to see if anyone in the street was known to us. Fred Turner was flagged up."

"Flagged up? Why?"

"It was a while back, before they moved to Millar Street. A few of their neighbours made complaints. Firstly about inappropriate behaviour, fairly innocuous at first. He'd wander over when their kids were playing in the street, start talking to them, then pick them up, cuddle them. Things that maybe in earlier times no one would blink an eye at. But the parents were none too pleased. Then he started inviting one or two into their house to play games."

"What kind of games?"

"Just toys and stuff."

"They don't have kids so why did they have toys?"

"Exactly. So the parents were even less happy and warned him off and that seemed to be that…till a little girl came home drunk. That's when the pitchforks and burning torches came out."

"What happened?"

"They called the police."

"The neighbours?"

"No, the Turners. They got there just in time. The neighbours had kicked the door in and were doing the same to Fred when the police arrived. They dragged them off. Then the accusations started. So, over the next few days everyone was interviewed, statements taken, but there wasn't enough. Kids don't understand the difference between playing and…Christ knows. He may have done things they didn't even notice, touched them when they were engrossed in the game."

"And the drunk girl?"

"She couldn't remember. He denies it. Says he just gave her lemonade, and then she felt dizzy and went home."

"He didn't take her home?"

"He didn't."

"But if-"

"I know. They interviewed him. He protested that it was all just innocent fun that had been misunderstood. He just liked kids, and as they had none of their own this was their way of, and I quote, 'giving love to the children of the world'."

"Does he think he's fucking Michael Jackson?"

"He's a slimy, arrogant cunt and he's as guilty as fuck in my book, but there wasn't enough to press charges. They knew the game was up though, and moved not long after"

I thought back to that night at Fred's, hatred building with the image of the vile, obnoxious creature slumped in its chair. I wanted to kill him. Then I remembered the lies. The failed business, the implied gangster threats. All bullshit. But they weren't Fred's lies. They were Samantha's.

"Did she know?"

"Who? The wife?"

"Yes, Samantha."

He looked at me, a trace of suspicion in his eyes.

"Hard to say. She basically repeated what her husband had said: she was there when the kids were playing. All very innocent, she said. Put it all on the parents' twisted minds."

"And the drunk child incident? Was Samantha there at the time?"

"She was out that night. She didn't get back until the police arrived."

"So she could be innocent?"

"Who knows? Why?"

"Just trying to get to the bottom of it."

Then the waitress approached and asked if we wanted anything else. Simon said no, so I asked for the bill, but I wasn't finished just yet.

"So you think Fred is involved in her disappearance?"

"It's a possibility, that's all I can tell you for sure."

"There was no evidence of anyone else."

"There's no evidence against Fred either. A complete stranger could have broken in and taken her."

"But there was no sign of forced-"

"So he picked the fucking lock, he wore gloves, he knew what he was doing. It happens."

I sighed. "So you can't be sure. There's no evidence. I get that. But what does your gut tell you."

"Fred Turner is as guilty as sin and I want the fucker in a jail cell. Clear enough?"

"Crystal," I smiled. "So how do we make that happen?"

"You need to find Mary."

My phone rang. I looked at the screen. It was Samantha.

CHAPTER 18

Now aware of her lack of personal hygiene and generally unkempt appearance, Mary approached Tesco nervously, her previous confidence at being able to blend in replaced by something more akin to paranoia. To counter it she took a deep breath and fixed her gaze on the pavement in front of her, walking at an even pace biased towards speed, not glancing up for a second as she entered, immediately turning sharp left towards the bathroom. As she did, the security guard, a relatively young but unhealthily obese specimen, looked up from his monitors, transferring his attention to the lone muddy child who'd now entered his territory. As she disappeared from sight, he yawned and returned to reality TV, Tesco style.

Mary quickly surveyed the bathroom as she entered. No one at the sinks and the first toilet cubicle occupied. She opened the third, closed the door behind her, sat down and waited. The bathroom was totally without sound. She sat as still and silent as she could, aware of her breathing, regulation of which increased the tension further. 'Was there anyone even there,' she wondered. But she waited, a puff from the automatic air freshener causing her to gasp before placing a hand over her mouth. Outside the guard glanced towards the corridor then back to the monitors, searching the aisles. Mary's tension eased at the sound of rustling clothes followed by a flush and the unlatching of a door. She waited until the tap was turned on, then unzipped her rucksack as quietly as she could and took out a plastic bottle. With the hand drier's roar she readied herself. Silence restored, she counted to five then flushed, unlocked the door and marched out purposefully to the sinks, listening for a moment before unscrewing the bottle cap. Positioning the bottle beneath the soap dispenser she pumped frantically, all the while listening for footsteps, head turning repeatedly towards the door. Eventually she was done, the bottle full and recapped and returned to the rucksack. She swung the rucksack round onto her back with practised ease, and with heart racing, exited the bathroom.

Mary stumbled as she almost ran into the guard, bouncing off his advancing thigh. They looked at each other, each momentarily shocked by the sudden intrusion of the other. The guard recovered first, reaching out to grab the girl as he stepped towards her before his face turned white.

"Don't hurt me," whimpered Mary. Then louder. "Please don't hurt me"

"I'm not-"

"I'll do it, just please don't hurt me."

Sensing genuine terror in her voice, the man raised his hands passively, stepping out of the girl's way. "It's okay, it's okay."

Mary saw the gap and ran.

The guard watched her go, squatted down head in hands, sweating.

"Christ."

Mary ran as fast as she could, oblivious to pedestrians and passing cars as she hurled herself blindly on through the busy, indifferent streets, not slowing till she reached the park, not stopping till safe behind her trees and bushes. Her back hard against the wall, she drew her body in as tight as she could and sat still, eyes closed, trembling, feeling the world closing in. But outside, the world continued, Mary's ripple hidden in an ocean of storms and riptides.

And her eyes remained closed as children played, parents yelled, dogs barked and joggers panted. But then she opened them. It was a voice, distorted, but discernible as a woman. Mary held her breath, pushing her back against the wall, feeling the wall push back harder.

"Passers-by spotted her run into the park, over."

"I've been most of the way round. No sign yet. Any kids reported missing? Over."

"Still checking that. Maybe she's moved on. Over."

"Maybe. I'll check the rest of the park and ask around. Over."

"Roger that."

Mary listened as the footsteps moved to the right, softly exhaling as they disappeared. She remained there, undercover, for three days.

CHAPTER 19

In the days immediately after my meeting with DS Black I did little to find Mary. Maybe because he hadn't given me anywhere to look. Any pointers to help locate her. But then if he had any I suppose he'd have found her himself by now. What he had given me was a working theory, albeit light on detail, and with that should have came motivation, the drive to find the truth and maybe Mary herself. Instead, however, what it had given me was the mental equivalent of a forty car pile-up on the M6. I had stayed sober, limiting the impact, but remained incapable of forming a coherent plan to move forward. Instead, I parked up on the hard shoulder of self-absorption listening to the same thing on heavy rotation. Not the X-Factors latest nail in the coffin of creativity, nor a song of any kind. It was a question that I kept asking but could not yet answer.

"Have I been fucking Myra Hindley?" I muttered to myself for the hundredth time. "I mean…is it possible? Is she capable of…?"

I seemed unable to finish the detail of the accusation as if saying it would make it true, preferring the lingering hope of doubt to certainty's despair. I tried to convince myself that they were a couple who seemed to live separate lives, so maybe they did then too. Maybe she had seen nothing or at least nothing she couldn't explain to herself, convince herself of, while Fred, the real monster, and hopefully the only monster, hid brazenly in plain sight. Isn't that what monsters do? Hide behind the rational impossibility of what they do? Or was she more like the neighbours of Auschwitz who knew nothing, saw nothing, heard nothing and smelled nothing. But didn't most monsters act alone? That's what my fingernails clung to rather than conceive of her as an active partner. That she had 'merely' turned a blind eye, unable to believe the truth. But wasn't I in danger of doing the same?

A buzz interrupted my self-flagellation. Another text from Samantha.

'I really miss you. Have I done something?'

"Well, that's the fucking fifty billion dollar question, darling. What have you done? And for a bonus ten billion, what did you know?"

I tossed the phone on to the floor and sighed a Guinness world record sigh, remembering an earlier text that Fred was out for the evening. Would I like to come round? I could do anything. Anything. Such a big playground, but one that now seemed littered with dog shit and broken glass. I poured myself another mug of coffee, a poor drug to choose, perhaps, but one driven by a desperate need for focus, if not a minor epiphany. Or I could brainstorm with myself.

"I can't hide for the rest of my life. I need to tell her something."

"You need to tell her to fuck off."

120

"Innocent until proven guilty?"

"And if she is guilty? If you have been fucking Myra Hindley?"

"That's a big leap. Well, a leap. We're not there yet."

"And you'll take the chance?"

"I'm not saying that."

"I know you, remember. I know the other question in your head."

"What question?"

"Fuck or no fuck."

"Well, it's no fuck, okay. But I can't hide here. I can't avoid her forever."

"So tell her to fuck off."

"But is that the best idea. What if…"

"What?"

"Keep your friends close but your enemies closer."

"Pump her for information?"

"Your words, but yes. Play along, get her to trust me. Maybe she's desperate to talk."

"She does hate Fred."

"She does. What other plan do I have?"

"Plan A. Find Mary."

"I can do both. But I can't concentrate on finding her without at least trying to find out the truth."

"Okay but…"

"Okay, I get it. Jesus, you're like Jiminy fucking Cricket."

"Well, no one needs a conscience more than you. Besides, maybe it's time you tried becoming a real man rather than a real boy."

Clenching my fist, I brought it down hard on my head, feeling as mad as I no doubt looked. And then I reached down and picked up the phone.

'Sorry. Phone been playing up. Looking forward to tonight. See you about 8.'

Send.

Buzz.

'Make it 7 xx.'

"Fuck."

Then seven came. I didn't even change. Draped in the irony of my Superman tee-shirt, I emerged, last meal waived, resigned to fate and her gallows. I stopped at her door. Her, as if unable to say her name, now seemingly as unspeakable as the deeds lurking in the shadows.

As the scales of justice swung between innocent and guilty I felt my finger move towards the bell, hoping for battery failure, silence then escape.

'Knock? I didn't even think of that. What am I like?'

But the ding dong only reached the first syllable before the trap door swung open.

"Come in," she enthused, almost dragging me over the threshold. "I like the tee-shirt. I'm sure you'll live up to it."

A brief squeeze of my balls removed any traces of ambiguity.

"Do you want a drink or do you…?" She looked upstairs.

"Let's have a drink first."

She looked surprised, even more so at the follow-up.

"Tea, milk, no sugar."

"Who are you and what have you done with Tom?"

She smiled but it was an awkward smile followed by a brief pause for the punch-line that didn't come.

"Well, I'm having a proper drink. The kettles over there. Help yourself."

My plan, such as it was, was to find a balance: a balance between friendly, but not fucking. The scowl etched into her face suggested my balance was decidedly off. I thought about joining her in a 'proper' drink but knew where that would lead. 'The middle way' as my old mucker, the Buddha, calls it. But with someone like her, where is the centre and how was I to find it?

"Don't be like that."

As she turned towards me I looked her up and down, eyes lingering on the ample breasts her bra generously offered up towards me.

"Alcohol can turn into Kryptonite," I said, forcing a smile.

She smiled back. "Well, we don't want that."

Kettle boiled and glasses filled, we walked to the living room, her leading, me following uncertainly behind. She sat, patting the couch beside her, crossing her legs, her shortest of skirts almost completely displaced by the fullness of her thighs. I wavered but bit down hard.

"You look nice."

"Nice?"

I looked down to her legs. "Well…"

"I thought you were avoiding me?"

"No, I…I'd just been thinking about what you'd said."

"What?"

"You know…Us."

"Us? That's why I thought you were avoiding me."

I took a sip to buy time.

"At first, maybe. I hadn't thought about an us, but…"

"But what?"

"Well, then I did. Maybe there could be."

Another sip.

"And maybe we should talk. Find out about each other."

It was her turn to sip, or gulp as it was.

"See if we're compatible?"

"Something like that."

She laughed. "Welcome to Match.com."

As she licked the rim of her glass I craved the moral ambiguity of alcohol.

"Maybe more like a first date," I replied.

"We're a bit past that."

"Well, we've got that out the way."

"Out the way?!"

"I didn't mean…Maybe we just got it the wrong way round, that's all."

124

"We're not sixteen, Tom. Fred won't be gone all night."

"You were the one who wanted to talk," I found myself spluttering. "And maybe you were right."

She glowered at me, confused and frustrated.

"And maybe I wasn't. I've been thinking about it too. I'm not going to leave him and run away with you. For better or worse, till death do us part."

'You've changed your tune,' I thought to myself.

"Has something happened?"

A glimmer of suspicion flickered in her eyes.

"No. I'd like to know you a bit better," I said.

"What? Take me home to meet your mum?"

"She's dead," I lied, enjoying the flicker of guilt on her face.

"Sorry. Even so."

Sips and slurps echoed in the awkward silence.

"Okay, Match Boy, what do you want to know? Favourite colour? Red. Favourite music? Old School Rave. Favourite film? *When Harry Met Sally.* I learned a lot from that."

I sighed.

"Don't get all insecure on me. I saved that lesson for Fred."

Perversely that actually made me feel better.

"Thanks. That's a start. Where were you born? When did you get married? Where did you used to live before here?"

"Does it matter?" she replied, uncrossing her legs.

"I'm just…I don't know what I'm." I sighed again, feeling any hope of getting to the truth slip away. I knew it was all or nothing.

"You mentioned kids before. How you couldn't have any."

She turned in her seat, her eyes reflecting the physical space now between us.

"What? You're offering to give me a baby?"

"Fuck no. Like I say, I'm just getting to know you. Do you want another drink?"

"Finally, something that makes sense."

I took her glass and went into the kitchen for a brief moment of escape before torment followed me in.

"You going to be all night with that?"

I poured her a generous brandy, then took a sip. I poured some more then took another sip and shuddered, adding a splash of lemonade, hoping the drink would loosen her lips before closing her eyes.

Her frown was still stubbornly in place as I handed her the glass.

"I saw the brandy bottle and remembered our first night together, how great it was."

"Well, aren't you sweet." She sipped. "No Babycham?"

"I looked. I couldn't see it."

"Isn't it next to the brandy."

"I didn't notice. I'll-"

"It's fine."

More silent sipping ensued as I waited for the brandy to take effect on her.

"You said not having kids-"

"Fuck's sake, Tom! We can talk all about 'us' later, okay, Honey. Right now I just want you to fuck me. Can you do that? I don't want Clarke Kent. I want Superman to fuck his little Lois Lane."

I knew now that talking, if it came at all, would only come after. As she wrestled with my trousers I wrestled with my conscience, beginning with how low I'd sunk as to view having second thoughts about sex with a child killer, or even a potential accomplice, as some sort of moral victory. Then came the notion of taking one for the team in order to extract the necessary information for the greater good. That seemed a bit of a stretch. As did what she was doing as she tried to 'invigorate' me, growing more frustrated and seemingly sadistic by the second.

"What's wrong, Superman. Tea got Kryptonite in it too?"

As she tried the kiss of life as a route to her own gratification I looked at her, trying to imagine the unimaginable, her hurting a child, or standing back smiling, laughing even, at Fred's cruelty. I searched but couldn't see even a glimmer of evil, only a woman, Samantha. That seemed to be enough, for now at least.

"There he is."

As she continued I lay back, surrendering to Samantha's quicksand of the flesh. Maybe I was due a night off. Maybe I was kidding myself. Maybe I was a selfish, heartless cunt. I could figure that all out later because right now I suddenly had Samantha's bare arse three inches from my face.

"When I said anything I meant it," she said in a low, husky, almost conspiratorial whisper.

Afterwards, watching her wipe her arse while I washed my cock in her sink, I felt post coital guilt pin the badge of conspirator through my heart. Had I been too hasty in her acquittal, rushed on by my own lust?

As she flushed away the remains of her adultery, Samantha smiled.

"Fred never would."

"A bit squeamish?" I asked as we headed back into the living room.

"Not a word I would use to describe Fred," she replied, sitting down gently.

I could see her eyes begin to go, the brandy now appearing a bit on the generous side. I hoped there would be time to get the dirt on Fred but sensed I had to act quickly.

"And how would you describe him?"

"Ha...If only you knew."

I felt sick. What had I done?

"He can't be all bad. You said he wanted kids. Anyone who loves kids can't be all bad," I replied.

"Yeah, yeah," she slurred. "Fred likes kids all right. Couldn't eat a whole one though. Haaahahaha! Couldn't eat a whole one." She roared, laughing again at her lame joke.

128

"If you can't have your own, did you never think of adopting?"

She seemed startled for a moment. "You sound as deluded as Fred."

"What do you mean?"

"He's started talking about that."

"What, adoption?"

"Yeah. Daddy Fred. Hahaha. The idea."

"You don't…"

"Never happen in a million years. Not after what happened."

I swallowed hard.

"What happened? What happened, Samantha?"

Samantha stared into space, lost somewhere in her own internal struggle.

"He says it would be different if he had his own, but it wouldn't. I know it wouldn't. He…He can't help himself. I thought he could. But then…"

"But what?" I asked urgently as I saw her eyes glaze over.

"That's why I stay, Tom. You're my Superman, eh?"

"Yes, your Superman, but what were you saying."

"Make sure he doesn't get out…"

"Out what?"

"Eh?"

"You said, 'Get out'."

"I didn't say get out, did I? Don't you go anywhere, Superman. The night is still young."

"You were talking about Fred."

"He gets a bit out…what was it…of control, that's it. Sometimes, just sometimes. Fuck him though. Didn't I say the night's young, Thomas?"

But the night was no longer anything.

We turned to the window as the headlights gate-crashed our party, tyres grinding on gravel.

She scowled. Then, as if suddenly awakening from a dream, panic fought through her sedation. "You need to go. Out the back. Quickly!"

As the car door slammed I left, a backdoor man once more, holding onto the belief of Samantha as protector, as a gatekeeper, while struggling to forgive her silence as the naivety of love. Trouble is Samantha didn't seem the naive type. But then neither did I. It would be a long night and I knew Jiminy Cricket and his dark hangover of guilt and shame would be waiting for me in the coming hours. Maybe I fucking deserved it.

CHAPTER 20

Samantha awoke the next morning startled by the shape lying beside her. Memories of the previous night were opaque to say the least, and Fred's presence rather than Tom's was somehow unexpected. She drew back the arm intended for her lover and lay on her back waiting for her memory to awaken, the ache in her rectum nudging the process along as she remembered Tom's seemingly angry lust as well as her own, his earlier distance and awkwardness, and the questioning.

"Fuck."

She bit her lip as she wondered what words had escaped them, trying desperately to remember exactly what she had revealed. As she sat up she turned to her husband, spitting on him as he snored. Cursing him for that and everything else. Everything she'd told and everything she prayed she hadn't.

She turned to face him, watching him breathe. How fucking dare he. She placed her hand gently on his throat, thumb feeling his pulse, strong and steady as if taunting her. She squeezed, just a little, just enough to take the edge off her rage, a little more as she found herself enjoy its pleasure, a little more before removing her hand as she felt him stir.

Samantha got up and walked to the bathroom finding an echo of pleasure in the previous night's pains but showering quickly, impatient to regain control. She dressed then absentmindedly prepared and consumed breakfast, barely noticing a bite, a sip or the casual tossing of dishes into the sink. Tom, however, held her attention as the charmer holds the snake's, hypnotising her, leaving her unable to be sure of his intentions or the veracity of her own recollections. She walked to the kitchen window, immune to her birds and their fruitless searching of empty feeders, beaks pecking complaints in avian Morse code as they glanced, side on, at the god who had abandoned them.

She sensed more than she could remember. She sensed his deceit. She sensed compassion, but wasn't sure for whom. She sensed fear but also that he'd gone past fear. Mostly she sensed his desperate need to know. She remembered his interest in children and in Fred. And she vaguely remembered responding, teasing, defensive, maybe. It was all so vague but she felt there was wiggle room: room to backtrack and correct if she could just speak to Tom soon.

But for the next few days Samantha could do nothing more than think. She couldn't stop thinking as fear tightened its unrelenting grip. Many times she'd held her phone, typed the words that would make things right before deleting them as her nerve failed. Now she sat drained by insomnia and stress, phone once more in her palm.

"Do you ever leave that thing alone?"

She grimaced as Fred sat down beside her.

"What's up with you anyway?"

"Nothing."

"Nothing always means something. You look like shit by the way."

Samantha stayed silent as Fred plucked at her last remaining nerve.

"So, have you thought about adoption then?"

"I have. I've thought about it a lot and…I think it's a great idea."

"Really," said Fred, no attempt to hide the shock in his voice. "You're being sarcastic aren't you?"

"No. I think it could really work for us. Bring us closer together. I know things haven't been easy for you since…"

"Things will change, darling. You'll see. This is just what I need. I'll stop drinking too. Straight away. You want a cuppa?"

She nodded and squeezed his hand, but her smile was no match for her husband's.

"I can't believe it. I'm going to have my very own little girl. Do you think she'll call me Daddy?"

"Why not."

"Yeah, she will. She'll call me Daddy and I'll call her Princess."

Samantha listened as Fred switched on the kettle and opened the tub where the tea bags were stored.

"How young do you think she'll be, Samantha?"

"I don't know. Depends on availability, I suppose."

"Maybe we could get a baby."

Samantha turned towards her husband but said nothing.

CHAPTER 21

As darkness fell on the third day, Mary's mind returned once more to the world outside the bushes, a world to which she knew she would have to return if only to eat. She remembered the dirt and the smell, and she remembered the soap that had almost been the end of her. Then she remembered Carnation.

"I'm so sorry," she croaked, her voice cracked from thirst, as she cradled her.

"It's okay, I knew you were there."

"I was scared."

"I know."

"Weren't you?"

"No."

"You're so brave. Braver than me."

"You're brave enough, Mary. Are you scared now?"

"Not so much."

"Ready to get washed?"

Mary listened intently. "Is it safe?"

"I think so."

"Are you sure?"

"Yes."

"Are you having a wash too?"

"No, I can't, remember?"

"Sorry, I forgot."

"Ready?"

Mary listened again, wondering what time it was. But it was dark and it was silent.

"Ready?"

"Okay then."

She reached into her rucksack, rummaging until she found the bottle of soap before crawling to the edge of the bushes, a nocturnal prey on high alert. Seeing no obvious danger she emerged, remaining in a crouched position as she walked the short distance to the pond, primed for flight at the first sign of threat. The pond was surrounded by a low wall, but high enough to be above head high when she climbed over and sat on the other side. She waited, hoping her breathing and heartbeat would ease, but a hooting owl sent both racing. She felt her body shake uncontrollably from cold and fear.

"I can't."

"You must."

Mary looked back towards the bushes where Carnation lay.

"I'm scared."

"I know but the longer you wait…"

Mary dipped her fingers into the water and wished she hadn't. She shivered.

"It's freezing."

"Mary."

"I don't want to," she sobbed, softly.

"You have to, Mary. Just do it."

Mary sat up straight, stung by Carnation's impatience. "I know, I know."

"Clothes too."

"It's so cold."

136

"Do it quickly then. Don't think about it."

"But how?"

"Take your clothes off and wash them first."

"All of them?"

"Leave your pants and vest. Wash them when you wash yourself."

"Socks too?"

"Okay, but hurry, it may get light soon."

Mary clenched her teeth and fists, breathing deeply. Then, steeled, she got to it. Jacket, hoodie, tee-shirt, jeans, each yanked off in turn, doused sparingly with soap, submerged in the icy water, washed and wrung dry. As the bubbles frothed and popped, her mind drifted to bath times long ago, filled with toys, laughter and warmth. Then feeling something else stir in the darkness of her memory, she switched it off.

Finally she wrung out her jeans as tightly as her eleven-year-old hands could, grimacing to draw all available strength to the task. Then it was time. Slowly, agonisingly, she slid into the pond, its waters seeming to freeze the very air in her lungs. With feverish urgency she rubbed and scrubbed at her body, its bones, and sinews hard, devoid of the luxury of fat, her tentative breasts hidden amongst the goose bumps. When she felt the worst of it was off she picked up the bottle of soap but then put it back as it dawned on her that the soap wouldn't get to the parts below the waterline. She got out and sat on the wall, scouting her surroundings, then poured a generous, Gypo-busting dose of soap into her hands and began lathering, beginning with her socks and feet. As her hands reached her pants she stopped, hands trembling from more than the cold, before continuing, working off the dirt that had clung for so long. Lastly her hair, her fingers rubbing each clump, feeling the grit dislodged from its hiding place, scrubbing her scalp, scraping each hair to its roots until Mary's hair emerged from its dirt-encrusted cocoon, each strand a silky red butterfly. The soap's sting brought its own tears, but Mary didn't mind.

Clean, she immersed herself once more in the water, rinsing away the hard-won soap, and climbed out. It had been so long since she'd washed that drying hadn't even entered her mind. But as she crouched half naked like Gollum by the moonlit pool it was a towel not a ring which assumed the role of 'Precious'. She looked back at the bushes as she shivered.

"I'm freezing, Carnation. What will I do?"

Carnation remained silent.

As Mary's body began to shake she grabbed her clothes and ran to the bushes, keeping as much of her body off the dirt as she could before sitting on her rucksack, feeling more miserable with every drip from her clothes running down her legs.

"Hang them on the branches to dry."

The slender branches bent under the weight but held.

"I think they'll be dry by morning."

"I th...th...think I'm d...d...dying," chittered, Mary.

138

Carnation sighed. "Sorry."

"I feel really clean though."

"I can see. You look beautiful."

"I think I'll be dead in the morning."

"Cuddle into me."

Mary picked her up, holding her tight.

"Better?"

"I…I…I think so. I th…th…think I'm sh…sh…shaking less now. I think I'll stay alive."

"Good."

"I'll sssstay aw…awake though. Just in case."

Mary sat shivering the night through amidst the rustling bushes and the piercing breeze, any chance of sleep lost to the ache of bones beneath her sparse flesh, scarred by old nightmares that didn't need sleep to stalk her.

CHAPTER 22

The morning after bathing the sun had shone with unseasonable warmth, but it was a warmth which took time to build beneath the leaves and branches of Mary's home. Every five minutes she would feel the hanging clothes, longing for dryness, sighing each time at the stubborn cold dampness she found instead. She herself felt no less cold, no less damp, her condition made bearable only by the mercy of numbness until eventually Mary tugged them impatiently from the branches, deciding they would dry quicker with bodily warmth and her body would warm quicker clothed. Then a voice.

"I think there's a dog in there, Dad."

"Yeah?"

"Let's look."

The voices grew closer.

"Can I pat it, Dad?"

"Steven! It'll bite ye. Come oan son."

"Daaa!"

"Come oan!"

"Okay."

As the steps ran then walked into the distance, Mary, released her breath.

"That was-"

"Stupid, I know. Sorry, Carnation."

"You need to be careful."

"I know."

Mary proceeded to get dressed quietly, dragging the sticking clothes slowly over her arms and legs.

"Are you still cold?"

"I think so. I can't really feel anything."

"It's getting sunny. You'll be warm soon."

Mary sniffed, first at the air, then herself.

"I don't think I smell bad anymore." She sniffed again. "I think I smell nice."

"You do."

"I'm going to stay clean. I'm going to wash every week. I'm going to stay clean and smelling nice forever."

Carnation purred.

"Where will we get soap now? The fat man might catch me if I go back there."

"Do you have any left?"

"About half."

"Maybe the fat man won't be on every day."

"Do you think so?"

"Maybe."

"He smelled."

"Who?"

"The fat man. Worse than me."

"Maybe he gets stuck in the bath."

Mary laughed quietly.

The leaves rustled as a breeze cut through her defences.

"So…cold. I hope it warms soon."

"It will."

"Carnation?"

"Yes?"

"Do I look weird?"

"Weird?"

"Because I'm still wet."

She held Carnation up to take a look.

"Well?"

"Not really. You'll dry soon."

"Carnation?"

"Yes?"

"Can I…Can I play on the swings?"

"Mary…"

"I'll dry quicker on the swings."

"Mary."

"I'm freezing."

"Mary, no."

"But I'm bored, Carnation."

"It's a school day, remember?"

Mary lowered her friend and sat her beside her.

"I'm sorry, Mary. People will ask why you aren't at school, maybe tell someone. I'm sorry."

Mary said nothing as she drifted back to school, to playgrounds and Miss Lang. She loved Miss Lang. Even the headmistress didn't seem so scary now. Some of her friends had hated school but there was nothing Mary wouldn't give to be there right now.

"Mary?…Don't, Mary."

But Mary had already started crawling out towards the sunlight, pausing only to look left, look right and listen in her own version of the Highway Code. Her face lit up as the warmth of the sun embraced her, lightening her steps as she

142

walked the fifty yards to the swings. Looking around she sat on the hard red plastic seat, rocking back and forth, her feet pushing gently against the soft rubberised mats that filled the play area. Its emptiness helped her justify her recklessness to herself at least, and perhaps ease the conversation with Carnation she knew was to come.

She pushed a little harder. A little harder still, feeling warmer with every inch closer to the sun she flew. Mary marvelled at the clunk of the chain and the whistling wind in her hair. She remembered Frankie Blevins, standing on the swings across from the school playground, swinging hard and so high Mary thought he would die. Then, at the bottom of its arc, kicking the swing skyward, as he skipped to a halt just out of range, not even looking back as the swing just missed his head before winding itself round and round the crossbar.

As she swung at a more cautious altitude, now clean, once more playing and with feeling returning to her body, Mary remembered happiness and recognised it once more. Slowly coming to a stop she ran over to the chute. Looking up to its summit she couldn't help but wonder if the one at the school playground had been far higher than this or whether that was a trick of memory. Frankie Blevins, she felt sure, wouldn't have gained his reputation from a slide like this, yet she remembered him whizzing down, usually head first, stopping impossibly close to the slide's end, inches from certain death. Mary examined its surface with a furrowed brow as she noticed the mud and grime coating it. No, her cleanliness had been hard won. She would not surrender it so cheaply.

Like a kid in a candy store, or a child in a playground, she moved to the roundabout, planting one foot firmly as she held onto the bar, kicking away hard from the off, propelling herself faster and faster, laughing with an old abandon as her hair flew in the cyclone of her making. She thought again of Frankie, her distant hero, lying down as the roundabout hurtled round like a spinning top, his head millimetres from the gravel below. She'd thought she'd loved Frankie Blevins and that maybe she still did.

As she tired she planted both feet on the deck, content to let the roundabout do the work, spinning freely until coming to an inevitable halt. As it slowed she spotted a woman walking along the path that lay between her and home, getting closer with each slowing rotation, noticing her face turn towards her…spin…she seemed to be slowing…spin…her eyes stern…spin…finger pointing…spin.

Both the roundabout and the woman stopped at the same time.

"You there!"

Mary said nothing, frozen in the spotlight.

"Shouldn't you be in school?" asked the woman, now walking towards Mary.

Heart now racing, Mary stepped off the roundabout away from the woman.

"I'm speaking to you!"

Mary ran. Only when she neared the other side of the park did she look back, slowing as she saw the woman now exit the park from the opposite gate. She stood, waiting to see if her accuser would return, scanning the park for other dangers. Eventually she walked slowly, cautiously, the way she'd come. As she reached the swings she stopped, glancing mournfully for a moment, her earlier play now bringing only the soft ache of nostalgia. She walked on, stopping at the bushes' edge for one last check before disappearing, trapped once more between the dirt and the stars.

"Don't, Carnation."

CHAPTER 23

Jiminy's hangover came as I knew it would, and it was a motherfucker of Samuel L Jackson proportions. When I left Samantha I didn't sleep, drowning instead, pulled under by riptides of doubt, guilt and self-recrimination. I felt like a skid mark in a world of shit, an apt metaphor under the circumstances, wondering how I'd gotten here, back to this place, and whether I'd ever really left.

But the next morning I knew I had to put her and Fred out of my mind or I would end up exactly that. I had been there once before and its memory was a fearsome enough warning. Instead I focused on Mary, and with the absence of a body after all this time I had to believe she was still alive. I would start locally. After that, who knew?

Sylvia didn't seem surprised to see me when she pulled open the door with startling speed. Her impatience continued as she ushered me into the living room, obviously ready to interrogate me, but she would be disappointed. I had decided not to share Samantha's revelations either with Sylvia or DS Black. It had all been a bit too vague but I sensed with a bit more trust I would get something more concrete. I knew if the police got involved she'd shut down. That was the story I clung to, happy to let it obscure my own unease and maybe shame.

"How did you get on with the police?" she asked, not waiting till I'd sat down.

"Not too well. Bit of a dead end," I lied knowing the truth would lead the conversation two doors down.

"Oh. That's a pity."

She sat deflated for a moment. "Sorry, where's my manners, would you like a cup of tea?"

I nodded.

As she disappeared into the kitchen I looked at the photo, feeling Mary's eyes almost pleading before Sylvia and her blessed tray saved me from myself. We sat chatting about nothing in particular for a while but inevitably we returned to Mary.

"So are you still trying to find out what happened?"

"Yes."

She smiled at first before her face became more serious.

"But how? Where would you start?"

"I did get the feeling from DS Black that he thought she was still alive."

"Really? Oh thank God."

"Just a feeling though. No more than that."

"I know, I know, but, it's something eh? Hope?"

"It is, Sylvia."

She watched me as I looked over at the photo again.

"Do you need to borrow the picture? To help find her?"

"I just need to copy it."

I held up my phone as an explanation. Her look told me more would be needed so I took the photo from its frame to stop the flash bouncing off the glass and zoomed in on Mary's face.

"Look."

I handed over the phone.

"Modern gadgets. That's amazing, Tom."

She handed back the phone and took the original from me, holding it gently in her fingertips like a sacred relic. I watched as she seemed to enter a trance before finally its spell fell away.

"What did the police say, Tom?"

Suddenly on the back foot, I hesitated. "How'd you mean," I asked cautiously.

"Did they think she was…ill?"

Sylvia tapped the side of her head, like many of her generation unable to say the words.

"You mean mad?"

"You can't say that, can you?"

"They didn't say. Didn't say much." I repeated. "Why do you ask?"

"Nothing, just something the neighbours said when she went missing."

"Who?"

"Them next to you."

"Which one?"

Sylvia looked at me, her attention uncomfortable as I suddenly felt myself become transparent.

"Just wondering," I offered, weakly.

Eventually I got the answer I needed.

"It was Fred."

I tried to keep my relief private.

"What did he say?"

"He said she used to talk to herself. Talk to her toy cat too. I saw her do that. But that's what children do, eh? I'm sure I talked to my Teddy. Didn't mean I was mad. But he would go on and on about it. He even did it once when I was talking to Ann and Gordon in the garden. Leaned over the fence, tried to be all sympathetic, but he couldn't help himself. Had to get his point across."

"What did he say?"

"He said it's a pity she didn't get treatment in time."

"You're joking?"

"No. Those were his exact words. Well, I didn't miss him and hit the wall. But Ann, she just burst into tears. That's the only time I heard Gordon swear."

"What about Fred's wife?"

"She was furious. I think she was scared too."

"Scared?"

"That he would get lynched. She didn't hang about. Dragged him into the house by his shirt collar."

"Good."

"Good?"

"I mean for Ann and Gordon. But no, the police didn't mention anything like that."

Sylvia seemed content to accept my explanation, returning the photo to its frame.

"So what now?" she asked, nodding towards the phone I still clung on to.

I shrugged. "Walk around and ask the homeless. If she hasn't gone far they'll be best placed to know, if I can get them to trust me, that is."

"But surely if it's a wee girl?"

"A lot of them have escaped from terrible situations and just want to hide. They wouldn't want to be found so they'll maybe think Mary would be the same. Helping would seem like being a grass."

"But…"

"Wee girl or not, that's just how it is, Sylvia."

I stood up, feeling far heavier than my fourteen stone.

"I suppose I'd best get started. I'll keep you posted but I get the feeling this could take a while."

"As long as something's happening there's hope, Tom. There's hope, eh?"

I left to find it.

CHAPTER 24

In the days that followed, the heat from that sunny afternoon had stayed with Mary, but transformed into a feverish bush-fire burning pain and misery through her body, as sweat turned to ice water in the morning chill. Her food was gone or perished, adding to the stink of a toilet that she now realised was too close. She wondered who else could smell it and whether she would die here, a thought that brought curiosity rather than fear.

"You need to eat, Mary."

"I'm not hungry. I'll be sick."

"You'll feel better, I promise."

"I can't."

It took another two days before the pain of hunger overwhelmed the pain of her illness, her stomach seeming to gnaw on great chunks of itself as she lay there, shivering.

"We need to find food, Mary. Now."

"Okay."

With what little strength remained, Mary crawled back out into the moonlight holding her body as clear of the dirt as she could, wiping it from her hands on the damp dewy grass. As she swung the empty rucksack over her shoulder, she remembered her last expedition and the joy she'd felt at the weight of the full rucksack on her back, but now its memory brought only weariness. She thought of the fence, of the bin, the walk and the danger. But she walked. Even as the earth tugged at her feet with every step, she walked. She had no choice.

Exhausted, she crouched opposite the wire mesh fence, forcing a now cursory glance left and right before staring at this impossible adversary.

"I can't," she sobbed.

"You can, Mary. Rest for a moment then…"

It seemed to Mary as though Carnation too had nothing more to give. She sat hoping that strength would gather of its own volition. Eventually it seemed easier to climb and fail than to sit and wait for hope. She threw her bag upwards, the sight of it clearing the fence lifting her spirits a little, before she began the climb, thinking of anything but the fence and the climbing and the wire cutting into her stinging cold fingers, her panic as her toes slipped from the mesh, desperate to hold on, to hold on and reach the top, another slip, fingers agonising, toes then secure and pushing once more until she was over, dropping to the other side in a bone crunching heap. She rolled over, soaked in pain but too tired for tears. As she lay, looking skyward at the top of the fence, wondering if she was trapped, she almost felt relief before hunger wracked her stomach once more.

"Once you've had something to eat, Mary, you'll fly over that fence. You'll see."

152

Mary got to her feet. The bruises were on their way but weren't here yet. She soon found the bin into which she'd burned the step but climbed up to find it empty. 'Were they all empty?' she wondered in panic. Had it all been for nothing? Was she to die here?

She clenched her tiny fist, banging the side of the next bin, its solid thud rekindling hope. She took out the lighter. Spark. Spark. Spark. Then finally flame. She held it to the hard plastic, watching it soften and burn, its fumes making her dizzy as she slowly moved the flame sideways, elongating a foothold as she had before, waiting for it to cool and harden before climbing up, looking in, marvelling and grateful for the waste of the world. Then she saw the sandwich packet and the flame licking the cardboard as it charred and spread to the next. Mary reached it to pull it out before it spread further, but she had reached too far. Upside down she fell into the darkness as the lid dropped behind her. She wriggled, trapped, trying to right herself as she smelled the smoke, the fumes, felt the heat thaw the ice from her fingers before bringing its own sting. Mary screamed, her frantic movements only stoking the fire. Suddenly the lid opened. Mary looked up as an arm reached down to her through the smoke. At first she drew back.

"Please. Let me help ye."

The voice was familiar. Mary tried to reach up before the blackness took her.

It was the smell that Mary sensed first. In her nose, her throat, her chest. Then she felt the arms around her. She froze at first before wriggling free. Pushing away from them. Away from the man.

"It's okay, Ah wis jist warming you. Guess yu're warm enough."

Mary felt her heart race as she sat opposite him, quickly realising he sat between her and the only way out. Then she recognised his face: the man in the church, the arm reaching into the flames. But he was still a man. She searched inside herself for the old pains but felt only bruises from the fall and the fever that gripped her.

"You're sweating a lot."

"You stink a lot."

"Well, we don't aw huv oor ain private lake tae bathe in."

"You were watching me?"

"Don't worry, ah turned away."

"You're still a peeper."

"Am I fu…I told yae. Ah looked away."

"A spy then."

"Just to make sure you're safe. Make sure you're okay."

"I'm fine."

"My ar…You're no fine at aw. You're no well. You've got the flu or somethin."

"I want to go. Let me go," said Mary, tentatively. She looked around. "Where's Carnation?"

"Who?"

"My friend."

"There wis only you."

"My bag," whimpered, Mary.

The man pointed to the corner. "Over there. Feels empty though. Must be a pretty wee friend."

Mary crawled over. "Carnation's my cat."

"Shit. I…I didn't hear anything. Maybe you better let-"

He watched as Mary tore at the rucksack, squeezing Carnation tighter than life. He smiled.

"She okay then?"

Mary nodded.

"Who's he?" whispered Carnation.

"I think he saved me from the fire."

"He's a man."

"But maybe-"

"He's a cunt."

"Carnation!"

"What did she say?" asked the man, not unused to such conversations with those in the throes of the DT's.

"Nothing, just that we should go." Mary looked warily at the man. "I think we should too." She sat silent and motionless as she watched him, waiting to see what would come next.

"I think you should stay here."

Mary tensed.

"See," said Carnation.

"You're ill. At least stay here till ye feel stronger. Then…it's up to you."

"I want to go."

The man heard the fear in her voice.

"I'm guessin you've been hurt in the past. A man's hurt ye. But we're no aw like that. Ah could never…Ah've got a wee lassie at hame, jist about your age. Ma wee princess. Ah could never…"

"So why are you out here? Why aren't you with her?"

The man sighed. "I just wisnae good enough. Couldnae gie her the life she deserved. No wae the drink. But she's got a new da now. Rich. She's happy. Better withoot me."

"I don't trust him."

"I'm so tired, Carnation. Maybe he's telling the truth."

"He's a man."

"So was Dad."

"And what use was he."

"Jist till you're stronger," repeated the man. " Ah've got plenty ae food for baith e us."

Mary looked at this stranger and felt the weariness in both of them.

"Just till I'm better."

"Mary!"

"Aye. Jist till you're better."

It took Mary a long time to fall asleep, what with Carnation's muttering, her own thinking and the fear that fuelled both. She tried to remember back. Hadn't some men been kind? School was all women teachers, some very grumpy too, like Miss Brown who'd nipped her arm for talking, then pretended she hadn't. Her mum had got cross when Mary had told her and put it down to Miss Brown needing a man, so they can't all be bad, at least some of them, some like her dad. He was a kind man, no matter what Carnation said, and Mary loved him. She'd tried to forget him, knowing how she must have hurt him, disappearing as she had, and couldn't bear to think of her dad crying. But she knew she'd had no choice.

But would this man be like Dad or be like him? How was she to know? Hadn't he said he was her friend too before his games turned to pain and secrets, trapping her and using her Dad as an unwitting accomplice, knowing she couldn't tell him the truth? No, better the memory of a little princess than see him look at her as she knew he would. Even a runaway princess.

Eventually Mary wearily surrendered to whatever fate ordained as sleep gently took her in search of peace. The man watched her from the corner of the room, eyes barely visible in the dark, oblivious to the damp rising from the cracked grey concrete, sucking away any warmth his blood tried vainly to circulate. He watched her breathe and the plume that rose from her mouth into the night. But she looked hollow and her flimsy jacket was no match for the ice in the air. He saw her frailty and her strength, and he saw his own failings as a father, wincing at a memory's sting, cursing Mary one second, loving her the next. He took off his coat and walked quietly to gently rest it on her. It was a good coat, he thought to himself.

A warm coat. Sitting back down he rummaged in his bag for his other jumper and pulled it over the first, struggling as it clung to him. Eventually he wrestled it on, and from his bag and its remaining contents he formed a pillow. But before his head had even moved to meet it he heard the nightmares begin.

At first she wriggled and twitched, as if squirming to free herself. Mary's moans turning to muted screams as she pushed 'it' away, only for it to return stronger. He watched her fight as he knew she had a hundred times before. Waiting for it to be over. Understanding now what he had taken on with a guilty gratitude. A moment's stillness came as it seemed to wane, returning to wherever nightmares go to rest only to awaken again, forcing her once more to lash out, scratching, kicking, punching as all the while he watched impotently, knowing he couldn't comfort her. As her struggle weakened and ended, her tear-streaked face hid itself within her tiny, curled-up body. Only then did the nightmare finally show pity.

As she rested he continued to watch over her, a little girl with nothing except a pink toy cat with a wonky eye staring straight at him. But now she had him too. Soon he and Mary were both asleep.

The next morning Mary woke first, disoriented by her surroundings and the coat that covered her. Then she remembered. She lifted the coat and checked her own clothes for signs. Shivering, she pulled the coat tightly around her.

"It was warmer in the bushes," said Carnation.

Mary said nothing.

"Feeling better?"

"No. Worse."

"Worse how?"

"I can't breathe very well."

Mary coughed a barking cough, feeling her lungs rattle in her chest.

"Did you do that deliberately?" asked Carnation.

"Don't be silly."

"Sorry."

"Why would I?"

"I think you like him."

"No I don't…I don't know."

"You liked Fred too, remember."

"How could you say that?"

"I'm sorry, Mary."

"You have to promise never to say anything like that again," she sobbed.

"I promise. I'm sorry, I just want to look after you."

"You do look after me."

"Forever."

"Forever."

"Fred was a bastard," growled Carnation.

"That's a bad word."

"But he was."

"Yes, he was."

"Was what?"

Mary smiled. "You know what."

"Say it."

Mary sighed. "Fred was…a bastard."

Carnation laughed. "Mary McDonald says bad words! Mary McDonald says bad words!" she sang.

Mary laughed. "Shut up, Carnation. You said them too. More than me. Much more."

"Who's Fred?"

Mary's face paled as she turned to the voice from the corner. "You're awake."

"Yes. Who's Fred?"

"No one…It's just a game we…I play."

The man neither believed nor pushed her. He knew who Fred was.

"How are you?" he asked.

"Tired. Sore. I can't breathe very well."

He thought about putting his hand on her brow, putting his ear against her chest, but knew he could do neither of these things. He searched in his bag and took out a tub of Paracetamol. Maybe they could find a use beyond his hangovers. Maybe he wouldn't need them at all. He saw her tense as he approached and reached out to pass the tub to her.

"Take two wi' a drink of water. Might make ye less sore. Cool ye doon."

She looked at the label suspiciously at first before recognising it as what Dad gave her when she had a sore head. Struggling at first, she undid the cap and shook out a handful, taking two, putting the rest back. She looked at him for a moment.

"Thank you."

The man nodded.

Taking out her water bottle she swallowed the pills, then the water, its fierce chill piercing her teeth. She shuddered.

"Cold?" he asked.

Mary nodded. No one spoke for a long time as their thoughts separated them. Eventually the man spoke.

"My name's Billy Moon."

"That's a funny name."

He shrugged. "What's your name?"

"Mary."

"Mary what?"

Mary didn't reply.

"Mary's a nice name."

Mary frowned at him. "It's no nicer than any other name."

'Why no ask her if she wants a sweetie and be done with it, ya fuckin edgit,' Billy thought to himself.

"True. No the best. No the wurst. But at least it's something tae call ye."

Mary nodded.

"I'm Billy."

"You said."

"Oh, aye, so ah did."

Billy stretched his legs out to ease the ache of the stone and the cold, his eyes nervously switching between the barren room and the girl, not wanting to stare, to scare, but simply to know.

161

"Are ye hungry? Ah'm never sure if you're meant tae feed or starve these things. I'm a wee bit oot ae ma depth, medically speakin."

"I'm hungry."

"Well, that's good, ah think. Maybe that's a good sign. Must be, eh? Aye. Must be." Billy smiled at her, allowing it to linger, seemingly reassured. "Good, ah'll go oot. Beg fur a wee bit. Bring us something back. Whit dae ye like?"

Mary shrugged. "Chips." She couldn't remember when she'd last had chips, hot ones anyway, and her stomach howled at the thought. "Yes, chips."

"Salt? Vinegar?"

She nodded before hesitating. "And tomato sauce?"

"Nae bother, Mary. Nae bother at aw. Ah'll be back soon. Just you sit there and keep warm…Unless you're too warm then…Make yursel comfy. I'll no be long."

As Billy left heading to the cold outside, Mary sat shivering in her own heat, the regular drip, drip of the rain drops falling in the dark all there was to break the chamber's hollow hush.

"We should go now. While he's gone."

"I can't, Carnation. I'm too…"

"Before he comes back."

"No. I just want to sit."

"But."

"You go if you want."

"You know I can't. I can't leave you."

"Then stay."

162

"But."

"I can't."

"But he'll-"

"He won't."

"You don't know that."

"Neither do you."

"I know enough. I remember enough."

"I… I think Billy's like Dad."

"Your dad was-"

"I don't care. I just don't care anymore."

"Remember."

"I don't want to remember. I want to forget."

"You can't forget."

"Because you won't let me."

"But I-"

"Stop, Carnation. Please, stop it!"

"I'm sorry. We'll stay till you're better."

She held Carnation close and soon both were soaked in her sweat, felt the rumbling of her stomach and waited in the cold and the pain and dirt for Billy's return.

Billy sat in his usual spot just over the border from Tesco. With eyes down and hood up to shelter from the rain and the disdain, he waited for charity's warmth to slip through the clouds into his battered old Costa cup. For some reason he thought of Stan, the dog he'd found wandering lost only to give away months later in a moment of desperation, feeling drug's hunger and the need to come back home, only to realise home was no better than down south. He felt the shame now as he had then, even giving a false name to the recipient as if that would prevent public knowledge of the uncaring cunt that he'd become. Stan could bring in the coin too but it was the warmth, the licked face in the morning, the friendship he missed now as bitterly as the wind that whipped through him as he sat with only memories of greener grass.

Coins and rain both fell into his cup, though not in equal measure. One he poured onto the pavement, the other into his pocket lest he appear too wealthy and therefore undeserving in the eyes of his charitable patrons. As he sat he thought of Mary, of her past and of their future, wondering what that could be…

Even with his hands burrowed halfway up his sleeves the wind still found them, nipping away at Billy's finger-tips like a swarm of enraged ants. He winced with each sting until all that remained to his senses was a numb throb, the fading pulse of a dying man. He looked down at his cup, full to overflowing with water, yet beneath glittered silver and gold. He just had to reach for it. But it was useless. His protesting fingers had deserted, leaving only four senses and they would follow suit if he stayed here a minute longer. He kicked the cup over, relieved to see the water spill and the coins stay put, before using whatever motor function he had left to get both cup and payload into his pocket. As the wind and rain lashed his face once more, he stuffed his sleeves into his pockets hoping the hands were still there. Counting would have to wait but, hypothermia aside, he sensed it had been a good day, good enough not to break a promise to a little girl. And so, pushing himself up, Billy headed for Mario's fish and chip shop, aching with every sploonging step for its shelter and warmth as much as its rich, greasy food.

As he entered, Mario's smile and central heating embraced him, a hint of heaven to ease the toils of life. Here he wasn't Billy the beggar, the waste of space, the blot, blight or any other 'B' word on the landscape. Here he was Billy the customer. He was Billy the regular and as such valued above the transients and tourists. It was he whom Mario depended upon to balance the books every month, a responsibility Billy was happy to accept along with the food that was bought and paid for, then savoured like the sauce he poured on it.

But Billy wasn't just one of Mario's regulars. Billy was, he believed, and he believed because he'd been told, the only one with whom Mario had shared his secret. The secret of Mario's second name. Many had guessed over the years with only a smile and a shake of the head for their efforts. Donati, Pelligrini, Conti, Rossi, Russo, Mancini, Costa, even Soprano. All thrown onto the pitch just to be kicked into the stands. But Billy knew. Billy knew that it was McIlvanney. He also knew his first name was Rory, son of Ewan and Winnie, and he was no more a product of Italy than 'Oor Wullie' or the deep fried Mars Bar. No, Mario and his lilting Latin accent were as fabricated as the billboard proclaiming five generations of deepfrying expertise and more gold medals than Sir Chris Hoy. But it was good for business.

The revelation first shocked then amused Billy, but he gave no thought to using it to his advantage. The gain of a life time's free suppers could never replace the status of paying customer and maybe 'Mario' had sensed this before unburdening himself across the deep-frying confessional that empty Tuesday evening.

Once in, Billy headed straight for the radiator, extracting his tender digits cautiously, slowly stretching them out towards the heat, always remembering the time he'd got too close too soon and, like Icarus, had come crashing down to earth. In that instance though, it was onto the black and white chequered lino of a Glasgow chippie rather than to his death in the Mediterranean. Still, lesson learned, and with the fainting bullet dodged, he felt his fingers thaw, working them in and out. With blood flow restored, Billy took out his Costa cup and counted out its contents as discreetly as he could before rummaging in his pocket for the day's earlier takings. A total of just under twenty-two quid. Billy felt like a millionaire.

"One ah minita, Billy boya. Okidoki?"

Billy nodded, convinced that there must be more to speaking Italian than sticking a vowel on the end of every word. He laughed to himself at a memory from the previous summer when an Italian couple came in and, on hearing Mario's accent, had engaged him in conversation in the mother tongue. Suddenly stricken down with laryngitis he responded with facial expressions and sign language, somehow managing to maintain the façade for a while by strutting behind the counter like a mute Mussolini. Eventually laryngitis transformed into uncontrollable hiccups and flying chips, giving him no choice but to hand him over to his deputy, wee Senga, on the grounds of health and safety, while he retired to the back room in search of a cure. And the cure came with the miraculous chime of the doorbell, Mario returning hiccup free and once again the only Italian in the chip shop.

"Okaya Billy, whadda can I getta for you ah, eh?"

"I'll have a fish supper and…"

Suddenly Billy froze. Yes, he could get her chips and sauce, but would she prefer a supper? Maybe she didn't think of that or didn't want to be greedy. Maybe she wasn't that hungry. He could get her one anyway, just in case.

'Just in case!? Do you know how much it costs for a fish supper, Billy?' Asked his inner miserable bastard.

Of course he did and cursed the nagging, whiney little cunt in his head. Then came the honourable compromise.

"Make that a fish supper wi two bits e fish and a bag e chips too."

"Who's di chipsa forra, Billy?" asked Mario, intrigued.

"Naibdae."

"Billy has a girlafriend, maybe?"

Billy's face turned ketchup red with what Mario saw as embarrassment but Billy knew to be anger.

"Naw. Nae girlfriend. Jist hungry," replied Billy.

Mario sensed to let it go. "No problemo."

'Finally you sound like a Glaswegian,' thought Billy, as he watched Mario decant the food onto the paper with practised finesse.

"Salt and vinegar on everything?"

"Aye."

Then another dilemma. Billy didn't like tomato sauce much.

"Fuck," he muttered.

"Eh?"

"Nothin, Mario. It' no you mate, jist…gies a minute, eh? Ah need tae think."

Mario waited and Billy thought and the answer came soon enough.

"Goatit. Salt n vinegar oan everything. Tomato sauce oan the chips. The single chips, no the supper chips. And a wee sachet ae tomato sauce. Better make that two."

Mario obliged, reaching under the counter for the sachets.

"How much fur the sachets, Mario?"

"Twenty pence."

"Each!?"

Mario nodded.

"Fuck, me." Billy looked at the sachet then at the piece of battered fish.

"Ah don't even know if two-"

"Howa abouta I givea you three forra forty?"

"Yer some man, Mario. Pride e Italy, so ye are."

Transaction complete, they shared a smile and a cheerio and Billy made for the door where the wind had waited patiently."

"Fuuuckin'…hell."

Finally sheltered from the scourge of the elements, Billy savoured the moment, oblivious to the relative damp chill of 'The Bunker'. He leaned back against the brick waiting for his breath to stop tearing at his chest while wondering what, if anything, lay beyond in the other room. As his breathing settled, still he waited, preferring no answer to the wrong answer. It took a while for courage and fear to swap shifts, but it was the memory of the chips cooling in the bag that pushed his back from the wall and his legs forward, his breathing now stopped entirely.

Mary sat where he'd left her, eyes opening at his footsteps, mouth smiling at the bag he held and the steam that rose like a heavenly spirit.

"Ah goat here as fast as ah could. Hope they're still warm. It's freezing oot there."

Mary just smiled, sitting up straight, her shiver now one of anticipation as the waiter approached. Billy sat gently beside her, nervously awaiting the flinch which didn't come. Emboldened he pulled the first package from the bag, happy that it felt warm enough, and handed it to her like a sacred offering.

"Salt, vinegar and tomato sauce. That okay?"

The nod, the smile and the glint were answer enough. He watched as she unwrapped it slowly, savouring her gasp as the contents were revealed. She picked up a chip, a smaller one, dipping it in a pool of sauce before smelling it, eyes closed to heighten her senses, dropping it into her open mouth, chewing slowly. Then another, bigger, faster, hunger's patience exhausted.

As Billy watched, he remembered his own and the extra fish. He opened it up.

"You like fish, Mary?"

Mary stopped to look, her eyes seemingly unable to grasp what she was seeing.

"It's okay. I got some for you too. Look."

He reached into his pocket and pulled out the sachets of sauce.

"I got three just in case."

He held them out to her. She hesitated before her hands tentatively reached out to take first the piece of fish, then the sauce as her eyes lingered on those of her benefactor, probing, knowing how easily cruelty can be disguised.

"Thank you," she replied.

Mary opened and spread each sachet in turn, pausing for a brief moment of admiration. But brief it was and soon her teeth were tearing savagely at the batter and the white fish flesh, accompanied by moans of bliss. Billy watched in awe at the demolition before joining in but never quite catching up.

When Mary and Billy were finished they leaned back smiling and satisfied, their stomachs fit to burst. Soon both were asleep and, as they lay, Carnation watched over them both.

CHAPTER 25

After my visit to Sylvia's it took me some days before I could get going with my search for Mary. Not because of distractions, Samantha or otherwise, nor illness of body, though maybe of mind and spirit. But in truth it just seemed such a daunting task. The sheer number of people to search out, talk to, plead with. I felt sure it must be thousands but finding a hard number was a task even I saw through as a blatant delaying tactic. But why delay? There is only ever one real reason. Fear. And it was the fear of failure that was most daunting of all. As I sat through those few days I saw that it wasn't just the fear of failing Mary that held me frozen. If I couldn't find her, couldn't save her, then what was my use, other than being useless? Was my future to be a barren wasteland of prematurely rotting middle age with only the finish line on the horizon? And what if I did find her? What then? Polish my medals? Tell everyone who would listen all about my triumph and let them draw their own inevitable conclusion that I was a wonderful human being. 'I'm not one to blow my own trumpet, but…'

But get over myself I finally did, dragging myself out of the front door and into my car, determined and hopeful. First stop was the local library to print a hundred copies of Mary's picture with my phone number which I could hand out to my homeless search team, my eyes and ears on the streets operating under the radar, outside the system. I felt like Pongo in *101 Dalmatians* and with only one pup to find how could we fail? I could be such an arse.

I don't know what I was expecting. I'm sure I'd heard somewhere that as much as money, the homeless needed and craved human connection. Conversation. Even just a word. But now it was my turn to be ignored, with eye contact nervously withheld or given reluctantly with the implicit understanding that my fucking off would be greatly appreciated. As I marched from street to street I felt my leg growl, my old war wound, or badge of stupidity more like. I'd picked it up on a trip to New York where I ended up being mugged. At first I'd told my tiny black assailant to go fuck himself, and then he drew the gun. With hindsight, 'Go on then' was a poor choice of words but you never think of that till you get shot, do you? Thankfully he wasn't the murdering kind and, satisfied he'd made his point, went on his way. Not without my wallet though. By this point I thought he'd made his point pretty well too. Anyway, back on the mean streets of Glasgow, I limped onwards.

It took a surprisingly long time to realise that people are all different regardless of sleeping arrangements. Some were suspicious of my attention. Fear turning to relief when I showed them Mary's picture, knowing it wasn't them I was after and that a simple shake of the head would make at least this problem go away. But there were those who wanted to help, who looked hard, their memories straining before disappointment or, in one case, anguish etched their faces when they couldn't place her, as if, like me, needing a purpose. But they'd ask to keep it, maybe for future reference, and hide Mary's picture away like a treasured possession. Maybe something like hope.

But I did get something. A lead.

"Try the City Mission, mate."

Having always viewed red lights as advisory, the journey didn't take long and I soon found a parking space close by, depositing a scornful, 'Aye right' into the meter. The Glasgow City Mission building itself was the kind of building that probably gave Prince Charles nightmares, much as Camilla does the rest of us. It was square. It was grey. It looked pretty new. I also couldn't help thinking it must have cost a fucking fortune. But what was I expecting? An abandoned, derelict warehouse with piles of straw and a hippie in the corner singing 'Kumbaya'?

It was very nice. A place for people to enjoy all-too-rare moments of warmth and safety, with support if they wanted it. I saw the cross, and the meals being served and felt angry at all the other shite religion dished out as each version lost its way, leaving only pockets of the old, uncorrupted stuff working quietly away almost unnoticed. As I

174

stood still, smiling in this safe haven of hope, a man approached me. In his early thirties, with blonde hair and unthreateningly medium in height, weight and dress style, he smiled back at me.

"I haven't seen you around before. Welcome."

If I'm being honest, 'Cheeky bastard,' was my first thought as I tried to remember what I was wearing without looking.

"I'm not…"

I tried to think of something I wasn't which wouldn't seem insulting. What I was seemed a safer option.

"I'm looking for someone."

His smile remained in place but I sensed its motivation change as someone pressed 'mute' on the collective remote control. He looked at me, weighing up his options before pointing to a door. Thankfully it was not the exit.

"Please, take a seat," he said, as we entered what was presumably his office, and reassuringly spartan.

"As you can tell our clients are a bit wary of…well, most people. But the authorities in particular.

"Eh?" was the best I could muster.

"So are you CID? Immigration?"

"Fuck no. Sorry. No."

"Then who? A private detective?"

I thought about that one, but remembered I didn't have a card. Then I remembered the card that I did have, but they were at home and anyway, no one trusts the press. I decided, given the current religious environment, to place my faith in the truth, albeit embellished wherever advantageous. I took out the picture of Mary.

"I'm looking for this girl. She went missing a couple of years back. I'm trying to find her."

"What happened to her?"

"I don't know. I'm trying to find that out too."

"Is she a runaway?"

I squirmed, suddenly and acutely aware of how little I knew and of that how little I could share. He shifted to even less comfortable ground.

"Is she your daughter?" he asked.

'Fuck, that's a big lie, Tom. Don't.'

"No. No. She's not."

"Then who?"

"I'm a friend of the family."

'Better. And you are, sort of. They just don't know. Definitely just a white lie.'

"I see."

'Aye, right fucking through me,' I thought.

"I can see from the people outside that this isn't a kid's place," I said.

"We do help children but usually as part of a family group. Runaways rarely come here," he said. "What is it you want from the mission? You must have come for something."

I decided on the short version.

"Could you maybe put the picture up on the notice board?"

"Of course."

"And could I speak to some of the people? Show them the picture?"

He gave me a searching look, maybe seeing something I never could.

"On one condition."

"What?"

"If they don't want to speak to you, you leave them alone. You don't push it."

"Thanks…"

"Peter."

"Thanks, Peter. I'm Tom, by the way."

"I know."

'Christ, you're good,' I thought.

Then he smiled as if reading my mind. "It's on the picture."

Peter watched as I went from person to person, mostly, but not all men. Their responses were polite but though I sensed a willingness to help they were generally of the, "Sorry, never seen her," variety. I left a copy of Mary's picture with each of them, just in case. Only one refused to take her picture. He seemed scared, probably of me, of being questioned. I didn't know and, true to my word, didn't push it.

I felt some sense of achievement as Peter showed me out, and also some jealousy. For a second I thought about asking if there were any jobs going. Then I remembered the cross…and the 'Fuck' and settled on thanking him for his help. As I stepped out feeling an afterglow of holiness, a buzz from my phone electro-shocked me back into the material world. Another text from Samantha.

I'd been ignoring her again. It seemed simpler, allowing me to be the 'Good Tom', searching for a missing girl, rather than getting stuck in the moral swamp of my less better angels. I ignored this text too, got into my car and drove home, flicking on the wipers to clear the rain and the parking ticket obscuring my view.

I sat in my chair staring at the screen.

'I KNOW HOW WE CAN FIX THINGS.'

Capital letters this time. This time being the fifth since I'd gotten home. I looked at the clock. Only ten minutes since the last time. I sensed desperation setting in but I was now pissed off. Having finally gotten focussed on Mary, gotten my lazy arse up and out looking, here I was distracted again. What did she mean, 'fix things'? Say it had come out wrong and she would explain what she'd really meant? Or offer a quick fuck to put it out of my mind or leave it in the past? Maybe she wanted to go to the cops and get it off her chest? For a mercifully short moment I even thought, 'Maybe she wants to have a baby with me after all'. That was when I sat the phone down.

But it kept buzzing like a fly one step ahead of the swatter. I typed one word.

'How?'

Send.

Buzz.

178

'Not like this. I'll come round later. Xx'
'Fuck that,' I thought.
'No. Too risky. Fred.'
Send.
Buzz.
'Okay, where? Xx'
I suddenly felt as if I'd entered a bad spy novel, thankful that at least a daffodil and a copy of the *Sunday Post* wouldn't be required.
'Tesco café, 2 tomorrow.'
Send.
Buzz.
'Okay.'
I looked at the screen quizzically. "No kisses?"
Buzz.
'xx'
"There we go."
I immediately wished I'd made it sooner, knowing that what little remained of my mind would spend the intervening hours spinning like Kylie in gold hot pants. I then thought about Kylie minus the gold hot pants. Ten minutes later it was all Samantha and what the fuck she was up to.

Time can be a cunt. Like when you think the clock must have stopped, you hunt for batteries in every drawer in the house, change them, only to find time doesn't move any faster. Or when it convinces you that the hands are now, inexplicably after years of fault-free operation, suddenly stuck in position, chuckling silently as they move freely under the slightest touch of your finger, confirming that you are an arse. Time can also be a teacher, reluctant pupil or not. You learn that someone (you don't care who) walks their dog at 3 a.m.. You learn that Sylvia snores, and Fred and Samantha don't have sex because she could never be that quiet. You learn that only shit songs get stuck in your head and that you are a Womble, something you are reminded of over and over again lest you ever dare forget. You promise you won't. Yes, time can be a cunt.

I looked over at the clock again. As if to confirm the previous statement it hung there at five past three. I actually thought about changing the batteries but I wasn't that much of an arse, so I lay staring at the ceiling for all eternity then furtively glanced sideways. The clock now resembled a Salvador Dali abstract. Seven minutes past three. I got up. In the kitchen I felt exhausted and made myself a cup of coffee to wake myself up, smiling at the irony. It was at that point I fell asleep.

The coffee was cold when I woke up. I knew this because the wet patch on my trousers was cold and it didn't smell of piss. I looked at the clock. Twenty past twelve.

"Fuck!"

Showered, changed and breathless I slowed to a walk as I entered Tesco, making my way along the aisle to the café. I saw her. She was wearing a short red dress and knee length boots which were made for more than walking. She'd already

spotted me and looked around self-consciously.
She seemed anxious. As anxious as me.

I sat opposite her, my forced smile in place.
"Hi."

"Can we go somewhere else?" she asked
immediately.

"What's wrong with here?"

"Too many people."

I looked at her suspiciously.

"I'm not going to kill you," she whispered.

"Good to know."

"There's a park nearby. We can talk privately
there."

The park was only a short walk from Tesco. The
kind of park that nice families take their kids to
before the local shits vandalise it, the council
repairs it and the nice families return. Currently it
was awaiting repair.

"Nice and quiet here," said Samantha, gently
stroking my arm as we walked.

Past a swing park, near a pond, we found a
bench clear of prying ears. Behind us a bush and a
red brick boundary wall helped maintain our
privacy.

I took a deep breath. That was a bad idea.

"What's that smell?" I asked.

"I don't know. I thought it was you. We can
move."

"No, it's fine. Let's just get on with it."

Samantha turned to fully face me, her expression serious, tense, like someone on the edge of a cliff with a decision to make.

"Are you pregnant?" I asked, almost hopefully.

Her expression didn't change. Her reply a curt, "No."

"This looks serious."

"Deadly."

I was even more curious now and suddenly a little afraid.

"Interesting choice of words."

"But well chosen."

"So you did bring me out to kill me?" I asked, my attempt at laughter choked by nerves.

She looked around. "What, here?"

"You're not Russian, are you?"

"You've been reading too much spy fiction, Tom, or watching the news."

"Same thing. Anyway, back on planet earth where you're not a cold, ruthless killer, why are we here? Is there something you need to explain?" I asked, hoping to push the conversation onto my agenda.

"Earth can be a strange place, and people die."

"Christ, are we back to John Le Carre'?"

"Fred. We need to kill Fred."

The words, 'Thank fuck for that,' didn't get past the thought stage. No words did as inside a dam burst, washing me away on cleansing waves of relief and joy. I had been right! But more than that, my instincts still worked. I hadn't fucked Myra

Hindley. I knew it…hadn't I? Christ, I could be hard work. But I decided to enjoy the vindication, at least for a few seconds, till I remembered the murder.

For ages we just sat staring, waiting for the other to blink first. Eventually Samantha did.

"Penny for them."

Bit cutesy under the circumstances, I thought.

"Why?"

"Why what?"

"Christ. Why kill him, of course."

"I don't even know where to start."

"Start somewhere."

"Because he's a fucking monster."

"What do you-"

"I can't live with him anymore. I can't live with myself anymore."

"So leave."

"That won't stop him. You don't know what he's like, what he's done."

"So why don't you tell me."

"I can't. It's too painful."

"But it's him, right, not you? You haven't-"

"No!" she wailed, indignation etched hard on her face before it slowly softened into remorse. "But I could have done more. Done something. I should have stopped him. But I was scared. Scared of what he would do if I backed him into a corner. So…I pretend to go along with it. You've no idea what he's like! What he's capable of!"

She seemed desperate to finally unload all those years of guilt. But I didn't ask, maybe because I didn't want to know, maybe because it wasn't the question on my tongue. I hesitated before asking it, afraid of what the answer might be.

"And Mary? What happened to Mary?"

"I don't know, Tom, I swear. She just disappeared."

"Why?"

Samantha turned away gazing into the middle distance to hide.

"Was it because of Fred?"

She nodded.

"What did he do?"

No answer.

"What did he do, Samantha?"

"I don't know but I can imagine and I have, night after night. Best to keep it out of your head, Tom."

But of course now I couldn't and I sat there dying at the hand of my own merciless imagination. I felt her gaze studying my own torture, maybe with regret. But I'd asked for it, to share in it.

"So why now? Mary's been gone for two years. The other stuff, how long ago was that? Why now, Samantha?"

"You."

"What about me?"

"I'm not alone now. I've got you."

"All that time, though, and you never-"

"Like I said, I was scared. I did try but Fred's..."

184

"You must have had other friends over the years, people to speak to, surely. I'm no Superman, no matter what the tee-shirt said. What aren't you telling me?"

She sat up, as if steeling herself, physically and mentally.

"Fred wants to adopt."

I felt sick. "He wants to adopt a child?"

"No a fucking chimpanzee. Sorry, I'm a bit...Yes, a baby girl if he can, though I'm not sure if he'd be bothered either way."

"Christ. His very own sex toy."

"We can't let it happen."

"So don't go along with it. Tell him to fuck off. Tell the authorities, the adoption people, anyone. You can st-"

Samantha stopped me dead as she pulled up her blouse to reveal a scar. It's once-angry redness faded but clearly visible, the implication obvious.

"He stabbed you?"

She nodded. "When things started coming to light I couldn't take it. I tried to stab him. But he took the knife off me. Then he laughed and stuck it into me. His eyes, I'll never forget that look as he pushed the blade into me. So cold. After that I was terrified of him."

I tried to take it in, struggling for words.

"But I've got you now, Tom. We can do it together. We can end this."

"How?"

"I don't know yet. We need to work out the details. For now I just needed to know."

"What?"

"Are you with me, Tom?"

I looked at her, this woman who had up until a few weeks ago been a stranger, as had Mary the invisible presence behind it all. I sat silently, strangely at peace for what seemed such a long time until the peace was broken by the word, "Yes".

CHAPTER 26

Samantha and I had agreed not to risk being seen together until long after it was done. The love-tryst-murder motive had long become a cliché and we knew the slightest whiff of it would have the police all over us. It was risky enough without being stupid.

All communications would be by text sent and received by pay-as-you-go mobiles purchased by Samantha with cash for this sole purpose. They were old, second hand, definitely not smart and therefore harder to trace. A burner phone. I was in the fucking *Wire*.

We'd agreed to leave it a few days. Let it settle down. I never quite figured out what 'it' was. Maybe the acceptance that I was to commit murder. Samantha must have had a similar view. Her first message eventually came.

'Are you sure you want to do this? xx'

'Yes.'

'You realise we'll be committing murder xx'

'I know. Why are you asking me this? xx'

'Just making sure. It's a big step. If you're sure? xx'

'Yes I'm sure. Let's kill the bastard xx'

'Sounds like a plan darling. Can't wait to be free of him. You had any thoughts how? xx'

'Does he have anyone who would miss him? Family?'

Oops.

'xx'

'Not really. No friends, no brothers or sisters. His mother's dead. Father has Alzheimer's. In a home. What you thinking? Xx'

'If we do it here it could be messy. Body to get rid of. Neighbours. Questions. Risky. Xx'

'So what's your plan?'

'You go away together somewhere remote. Highlands maybe. Xx'

'Go on, xx.

'I follow you up. You go out for a walk together. Then we do it. Xx'

'What? Xx'

'?? Kill him of course.'

'Sorry. I meant how. Xx'

'Don't know. Figure that out nearer the time. Xx'

'You must have some idea. Xx'

'Does it matter? Xx'

'I just want to picture him suffer. Xx'

'A gun would be good. Less risky than using a knife or a hammer. Xx'

'A hammer? OMG seriously? You could do that? Xx'

'If it came to it. Xx'

'I so want to fuck you right now babe. Xx'

'Hammer it is lol. Xx'

'When? Xx'

'That's up to you. Xx'

'Okay. Leave it with me. Love you so much. Xx'

'Speak soon. Xx'

Hammer? I scrolled through the messages wondering who the fuck had been typing. I couldn't kill someone with a hammer, fuck or no fuck. I was no monster. I'd just got carried away, I reasoned.

'Is this the real life, is this just fantasy,' interceded Freddie.

"Fuck knows," I replied.

But I had to come up with a different methodology. Less brutal. Less messy. I was feeling squeamish already just picturing it, but as the nerves began kicking in they brought along a small epiphany.

"Drug him with my meds!"

Thank you, brain. Sedate, but then what? Stab him? Strangle him? Suddenly the hammer seemed the easier option. Or an overdose? Better. But if he wakes up?

"Fuck."

Something to think about, but not now.

I scrolled through the Google news feed on my phone as a distraction, stopping to admire a picture of a beautiful, sexy girl in a bikini before I noticed the words, 'Found dead yesterday'. Christ, there's a mood breaker. So I switched to the TV. About a hundred channels later I settled on ex-leper Michael Palin's *Around the World in Eighty Days*. Alexandria looked nice.

The next day, I put revenge on hold to continue my search for Mary, pissing rain or no pissing rain. I decided to head to one of the city's hostels thinking that would be like shooting the proverbial fish in a barrel. It was also indoors.

The Bellgrove Hotel was a fucking dump and that's sugar coating it. In a gesture of misplaced pride its name was emblazoned in large red letters, still intact only because no self-respecting letter thief would come near it and its clientele were too pissed to successfully climb a ladder. The next thing I noticed was that the adjoining building was an off-sales. I had to doff my cap to the genius of that piece of cynical opportunism, wondering if it was part of the Virgin Group. Outside the 'Hotel' entrance, the cream of the Gallowgate were huddled under the canopy smoking roll-ups, swearing and agreeing.

"Fuck's sake."

"Aye."

"Bit of a cunt, eh?"

"Yer no wrang, Danny."

"Fuckin sure ah'm no."

As I approached them they shifted nervously, puffing harder on their cigarettes as if to hide behind the cloud of smoke.

"Hink that cunt's CID?" muttered one.

"Na, too wet. They cunt's don't get wet n he's sploongin'," came the reply.

And I was.

"Alright boys," I offered as an introduction.

190

Unimpressed they went back to their roll-ups, hoping their collective snub would be sufficient and off I would fuck. But I persevered through their toxic mix of nicotine, BO and hostility until one man turned to face me. He looked old but was probably much younger, something weird about him too. Then I realised he had boot polished his bald head black. He looked a bit like Wayne Rooney.

"Whit dae yae want?" he asked in a tone that said, 'Stop staring at ma heid, ya cunt.'

As he did a few other heads turned towards me, happy to spectate if not participate. I pulled out Mary's picture, deciding to keep it simple.

"I'm looking for her. She's disappeared."

"So whit yae comin here fur?"

"Well, if-"

"Think we're aw paedos?"

"No, if she was living on the streets I thought…"

"Wan ay us wid huv lifted hur?"

"No, that's not what I'm saying."

"So whit ur yae sayin?"

I thought back to the City Mission, missing its tranquillity, sensing the spirits here were not of the holy variety. But even on the streets with all its hardship and struggle I'd found a kindness in the people there. Here, however, was a place of lost souls spreading a bitter hardness and it seemed to be contagious because suddenly I hated the fuckers. I was glad they'd been dumped here. It was where the bastards belonged.

"Jesus Christ," I muttered. "Look ya bunch ae wasters, has anybody seen her or not?" I asked holding the picture up accusingly.

Now I seemed to have their full attention. They had all now turned towards me, slowly edging in with a common hostility. Their de facto leader spoke.

"Whit did you say, cunt?"

I froze, deaf jokes on hold as the old me returned to shit himself. But the Lord works in mysterious ways.

"I said, Jesus Christ, my lord and saviour, has sent me here amongst you to find this child and to offer salvation to any who would seek it. Who amongst you will join me in prayer for the strength to do God's work? 'Suffer the little children to come unto me,' said the Lord then and he doth so again this day. Who will join me. Will you, brother?"

"Eh, na, yer fine pal," said the leader as he and his troops about-turned, heading for the exits.

I thanked Fuck and the Lord in equal measure then, realising I was no Billy Graham, I decided to end my ministry there, sensing perhaps that all that was on offer at the Bellgrove Hotel was sticky carpets and carbon monoxide poisoning. I did briefly wonder if there were any ex-hit men hidden amongst the residents who'd fallen on hard times but could still do a turn with regard to the Fred situation, but they didn't seem the most reliable of types.

192

So, like a good Christian soldier, I marched onward, thankful it was not to war but back to the streets, sploonging, hopeful and determined to find Mary.

CHAPTER 27

The next few days were a bit of a blur as I walked mile after mile looking for her while thinking of murder. Every day Samantha texted looking for an update on my plans, with each one distracting me further from finding Mary and feeding the growing sense that she was gone, that searching was futile as I drew blank after blank, leaving my imagination to fill the empty spaces with tales and pictures of every way a sweet young girl could meet her end. If Samantha's plan was to transform hope into simmering despair and then to boiling murderous rage it was working.

Another text came.

'Well? xx'

"Fuck's sake!"

Maybe women are right. Maybe we can't multi-task. Not with simultaneously saving and taking lives at least, so, with a new sense of urgency, I had to decide. How was I to commit murder? It had to be simple, so was going away somewhere the best option? Wasn't there more chance of being seen on CCTV?

Another fucking text. I felt my grip tighten on the phone.

'Are you chickening out? I need to know Tom. xx'

Suddenly so did I.

'No. I think going away is too risky. We do it here. Your house. Then dispose. Xx'

'Thank you Tom. I thought I'd lost you. You're right. Less risky. How? Xx'

'I have sleeping pills. Mix in his drink. When asleep strangle. Xx'

'With your bare hands? Could you? Xx'

'I'll use a cable tie. Easier. He's a monster. He can't get away with what he did to Mary or do it to anybody else. Xx'

'When? Xx'

'Tonight. Invite me round for drinks at 8. Xx'

'I can't believe we're doing this. Xx'

'Me neither but we are. He has to pay. Xx'

'I love you, Tom. xx'

Christ, I winced.

'See you at 8.'

'xx'

And so it came to pass that I, Tom Wilson, ex-social worker and of utterly unsound mind, found myself standing there in my living room, murder kit in my left pocket and heart pounding in my chest. But still I wondered.

The clock said eight. The clock could fucking wait a minute.

Buzz.

'Ready. Xx'

No question mark, just a statement of fact. So I added a question mark of my own and waited for my answer.

I didn't have long to wait after I rang the bell. She must have seen me or my shadow outside, blurred by the door's opaque glass and my own nervous vibration. She opened the door taking a moment to observe me, to gauge my state of mind and my suitability for the task. She winked and nodded me inside, her arm slipping round my waist with a gentle squeeze as she led me to the living room. I felt her confidence but struggled to share it. Inside Fred sat in his armchair. He looked over, smiling at me, smiling with that mouth, the one that had kissed Mary and Christ knows what else. His hair hung lank and greasy, flecks of grey, hints of aging, just not quick enough.

"Come in, Tom. Sit yourself down."

I sat in the chair opposite wondering what it would be like now that the monster was revealed. I knew then the answer to the earlier question was yes.

"Glad you could make it. I knew you would."

"How's that?"

"Another go at Samantha. You couldn't resist that now, eh?"

I said nothing, enjoying the little joust knowing I had already won. For now I was content to savour the pain behind the transparent bravado.

"Don't worry, Tom. It's okay, we're all adults here."

"We are that, Fred. All grown-ups."

'No fucking children here!' I longed to scream, but now wasn't the time.

Samantha's head appeared from the kitchen.

"You want a drink, Fred?"

"Is the Pope a Catholic? Does a bear shit in the woods? Are you fucking the neighbour?" replied Fred, his voice echoing with hollow laughter.

I tensed, ready to lunge at him, but Samantha intervened.

"Tom! You want to show me how you like your drink?"

Her eyes gripped me, dragging me from disaster to the kitchen, one last drop of Fred's bile slipping in behind as the door closed.

"Remember and wipe the work-tops when you're done, sweetheart."

I looked at her. "I don't know how you've put up with his shit for so long."

She reached out holding my face in both hands. "Not much longer now."

I nodded and took the wrap of paper from my pocket.

"I poured out the capsules earlier. There's enough here to put a rhino to sleep."

She took it and poured the contents into a glass.

"Do you think he'll see it?"

"It'll be fine with rum. Trust me."

"Okay. You go in. If we go in together it'll make him worse."

"I doubt that."

"Go."

"Okay."

I sat back down. Fred seemed barely to notice. When he did, a simple, "That was quick," was the limit of his interest. Christ, he was pissed already. This was going to be easy.

A moment later Samantha appeared carrying a tray with three drinks.

"I was just saying to Tom there, you finished him off quick. Bet your cunt's still aching for it."

"Just drink your drink, Fred, leave the small talk to me."

"I doubt if Tom's interested in what I've got to say anyway. Ain't that right, Tom?"

"Probably."

I watched as he took a generous gulp, then another.

"So how's the job hunting going?" asked Samantha.

"It's not really started yet. Been a bit busy."

"Busy?" snorted Fred. "Not too busy to claim fucking benefits, I'll bet."

"I haven-"

"Paid for with my taxes."

"Your taxes? What do you do again, Fred?"

"I've worked all my fucking life I…never claimed…penny," he slurred.

"But I though you were-"

"Setting up…new business."

"Really? What kind of business are you setting up?"

"A family busi…"

Fred's head fell forward, then snapped back, his eyes scrambling.

"Didn't she tell you then? Between…all the fucking?"

198

"What?"

"Havin…baby, mate. Beautiful little…girl."

Then he was gone, his drooling the perfect sign-off. I looked over to Samantha. She stood up and walked slowly towards me and clasped my hands in hers.

"Do it," she whispered.

"You go outside. No need for you to see this."

She kissed me tenderly on the cheek. "Thank you," she sighed, turning, seemingly lost until I pointed to the hall.

I was suddenly alone with all the monsters of the night and the uncertain terror of my own future. A stranger with a piece of plastic who felt he had no choice, only a job to do. I looked at the cable tie. I even remembered when I'd bought it. B&Q. Must be three years ago. They'll come in handy, I'd thought. Christ. I remembered pulling them tight on the wheel trims of my Astra. The feeling of nipping them up just that bit tighter. But Fred was no wheel trim, yet I was his executioner. I watched his chest rise and fall. I listened to the breath, the hint of a snore. I remembered the little girl's past and those to come. Most of all I remembered Mary. I took the cable tie, looped it, inserted the tail just inside the gripper, walked to Fred and placed it over his head like the hang man's noose. Then-

"Stop, Tom! Don't!"

I turned towards Samantha's voice and saw her, saw the camera pointed at me, as I stood ready to murder her husband. Then she lowered it and switched it off.

"Okay Fred, darling. It's done."

As Fred 'regained consciousness' I didn't even notice the cable tie slip through my fingers as he tossed my now pathetic murder weapon contemptuously aside, his face distorted in a hideous caricature of gloating.

As the world seized to a grinding halt, "What the fuck?" was all I could offer in response. They seemed to revel in their answer, firstly with laughter, then when that was exhausted, and it took a long fucking time, with words to match.

"Did you seriously think I loved you, Tom? A nobody like you?"

"But…" I looked at Fred. "Him?"

"You haven't seen the real Fred. I thought I'd lost him forever. But then I saw that look in his eye return and with it the only man I've ever truly loved. The man who takes whatever he wants without kow towing to petty morals."

"So you knew?"

"Knew?! I helped. And I watched. I lived to serve this man."

"Who the fuck are you?"

"Ours was a truly special relationship, Tom," purred Fred. "And will be again."

"And what about when I was fucking her?"

"She has her own needs. It would be churlish to restrain them. We enjoy a bit of drama and I have to say you've excelled yourself tonight, Tom. I didn't think you'd go through with it but she can be very persuasive. And that, my friend, can be very useful."

"Jesus Christ."

"You won't find him here, Tom, anymore than Superman. Hahaha."

I sat down before I fell, struggling to take it all in.

"He fucking stabbed you!"

"Actually that was the surgeon, when he removed my appendix."

How could I have been so stupid? I turned to Fred.

"So she helps you to…" I couldn't utter the words. "These are kids, for God's sake."

"Well, if God made me this way, who am I to disobey?"

"You twisted fuck. And you?" I couldn't even speak her name. "You're…"

"What? A woman?"

"Yes! You should be better than us. Certainly better than him."

"Fred's a great man, or he was until that little bitch nearly ruined everything. But she's not coming back. Now we can go back to how things were, or even better. I'm sure he'll make a wonderful father."

Then the fucking wink.

"That's not going to happen. I'll make sure of it. I'll be going straight to-"

"You'll be going nowhere," sneered Samantha, tapping the camera. "To answer your original question of what the fuck is going on? You being charged with conspiracy to commit murder. That's what'll be going on if you decide to be stupid."

"What? Bullshit!"

"All the texts, Tom. You, my lover, offering to kill my monster of a husband so we can be together.

"But...what about you? You'd be sending yourself to jail."

"But they'll see from the texts you took the lead, made the plans."

"I'll just deny it. Burn the phone."

"You mean this phone. The one that was in your jacket pocket with your fingerprints on it? And then there's this."

She waved the camera.

"This shows I changed my mind."

I stood shaking my head. "Nah, they'll see it as a set up. Why would you even be filming it?"

"Because you wanted a souvenir. But I couldn't go through with it, no matter how much you pushed me. That's what they'll see. That's what I'll make them see."

"But-"

"You can say all you want about child abuse. They'll see that as just a big lie. A cover story to save yourself. No, Tom, I'm afraid, 'Lover tries to kill husband' is far easier to believe, and the police will always take the easy option. You know that, Tom. It took them five minutes to write off Mary as a run-away."

Where my head had swum it now sank without trace. They were right. There was no evidence relating to Mary. There was, however, plenty of me as a would-be murderer.

"So just keep your mouth shut, Tom, and we all just get on with our lives," said Fred coldly.

As they both waited on an answer to Fred's implicit question I said nothing. But I had to know.

"And Mary, what really happened? The truth."

"As Jack Nicholson would say, 'You can't handle the truth'. But here's as much as you need to know. She actually did just run away."

"So she's not…"

"She was alive the last time I saw her."

"You expect me to believe you?"

"It's the truth, Tom. Paw promise, as she used to say. But I can't see her still being alive on her own. There's some bad people out there. She was safer with me, but kids, you just can't tell them, eh?"

I wanted to kill him now more than ever. I wanted to cut the bastard to pieces and make that fucking bitch watch before it was her turn. But I believed him about Mary; believed she was out there, and I knew there would be a better way. For now they had all the answers

She looked at me as if now growing bored. "Go home, Tom."

So I did, to find some answers of my own.

CHAPTER 28

Mary pulled down her jeans and pants, senses on high alert as she squatted in the designated girls' room. Glints of light pierced the blackness casting dark shadows and darker memories. Exposed and vulnerable once more, she listened for footsteps, men's footsteps, following her, their breath close by. She waited until she was sure before she dared reach the point of no return. Finished, she wiped and hastily tugged her clothes back into position.

Billy didn't look up when Mary returned, feeling her lingering suspicion and accepting it. Her crackling cough broke the silence as she dumped herself heavily onto the floor.

"Feelin any better?" asked Billy.

Mary shrugged before following up. "Don't know."

Billy nodded anxiously. He knew. If anything she was getting worse. He reached over and picked up his flask, filled that morning at the City Mission.

"Ye want some tea?"

Mary shook her head.

"It'll help ye. Wash down these too," said Billy, shaking the Paracetamol bottle.

Mary looked at him and said nothing.

"Ye don't have tae if you don't want, but-"

"Okay."

"Okay what?"

Mary tensed. "Okay, please."

"Naw, naw, ah didnae mean it that wi. Ah jist meant…Did yae mean okay ah want them, ur okay but ah don't want them?" said Billy, hands open and pacifying. "Sorry, hen. Yae dae want them, eh? Here."

Billy poured the tea and passed it over with the tub, happy to now sense bemusement rather than fear. She took them hurriedly before settling back and pulling Billy's blanket over her, warming her hands on Billy's flask as she sipped the hot liquid.

"You're getting too dependent," whispered Carnation.

Mary looked over at Billy who lowered his eyes.

'When I'm better, Carnation. We agreed.'

"But when?"

'I feel terrible, Carnation. Soon though. Soon.'

"Okay but don't say I…Soon then."

Billy watched as Mary stared at her pink toy, her face reflecting troubled thoughts within. He was about to offer a penny for them but knew that was a doomed transaction. Then her burden seemed to lessen amidst her sickness, but only momentarily as another cough broke the silence.

"Mary?"

"What?"

"Can ah jist put ma hand on yur foreheid?"

Mary felt fear stalk her as she sat rigid, apprehensive and silent.

'Told you,' whispered Carnation.

"Ah jist want tae see how hot yae ur. How no well. But ah'll no dae it if it's no okay. Okay?"

Mary nodded. Billy felt déjà-vu.

"So it's okay?"

Mary nodded again. Billy took a breath, holding it as he slid slowly towards her, raising his hand, placing the back of his fingers gently on her forehead. He winced inside as he felt her burn, hoping he'd kept its secret from her. But in the thinking his hand lingered too long and Mary drew back warily.

"Aye, yur still a bit hot," said Billy, sliding back to his earlier distance. "I'll go oot later and get ye some mair medicine. That'll sort ye," he said unconvincingly.

Billy waited until Mary was asleep before he allowed himself to think about her, lest an unguarded look or furrowing of the brow betray him. But now as she lay seemingly at peace he allowed his eyes to look upon her and acknowledge how much she looked like his own daughter, long lost to him but from his heart never far strayed. Many had been the prayer to the god of second chances since he'd seen this girl, first at Tesco, then the church, then every day from afar, praying for her safety, then more. But with every cough and moan and every cry in the night he felt family life crumble for a second time. His innocence this time round offered no shelter from the pain. But he clung on to hope like a life belt, and maybe denial too, anything to avoid sinking into the blackness as he had before, and from which there may be no way back a second time.

Anxiously he stood up.

"Goodbye, my Mary."

Billy then went in search of miracle cures leaving Mary to her dreams.

"What's the matter? You were better the last time."

"It hurts."

"It gets easier."

"I don't want to again."

"I thought we were friends?"

"We…I'll tell."

"Tell what?"

"Tell Dad I don't want to."

"Your dad? He'll just think you're dirty. Is that what you want your mum and dad thinking? That their little Mary's dirty?"

"They wouldn't."

"Ha. You think your dad would believe anything you say. Your dad thinks you're nuts. Always talking to imaginary friends. How old are you?"

"Carnation *is* my friend."

"And who gave you that friend, eh? Me. To watch over you, keep you safe at night, and this is how you repay me. Not very nice, eh?"

"My dad keeps me safe."

"You know he's sending you away, don't you?"

"You're lying."

"You're going to where all the mad people go. The nut house. The loony bin. Yeah, that's right; I can see you've heard of it. Do you know what they do when they get you in there? They open up your skull and then they cut a bit of your brain out."

"No! No, I don't want to go!"

"Calm down. Calm down. Maybe I can help. Maybe I can talk him out of it. But you have to help me. Stop all the talking to toys shit for a start. Then he might think it was just you being a silly little girl."

"Please."

"It's okay, that's what friends do. They're good to each other. Keep each other's secrets. And we're friends aren't we?"

"…Uhuh."

"And you're not a silly little girl, are you?"

"No."

"That's right; you're a big girl…Uncle Fred's big girl."

CHAPTER 29

The next few days were drenched with hate. Firstly for the evil going about its business next door as Fred prepared for the unfettered liberation of his perverted distortion of parenthood, serenaded by his accomplice's battery-fuelled wailing, mocking me through the mosquito net of a dividing wall.

Secondly, well, that was even closer to home. That was directed at the coward in the mirror who hesitated to pick up the phone and call their bluff, risk all, even a guilty verdict to save an innocent child. My trembling hands held onto the belief that I wouldn't let it get that far, that I'd make the call before they crawled helplessly across the threshold into Fred's lair. In the meantime I could use what remained of my physical freedom to save another child. The one still out there.

That was the story I told myself. I wasn't sure whether I believed it and maybe it didn't matter, not yet anyway. The only glimmer of light in a seemingly endless night lay in Fred's admission that he had in effect lost her, that Mary was the one who got away. But to where and to what? Frying pans and fires? In truth I had begun losing hope, feeling it haemorrhage away with each passing day, each blank face giving tacit permission to give up. But not yet.

My hopes rose when Emma had called unexpectedly. A woman had reported seeing a child matching Mary's description playing truant at a local park. The same park where I'd gone with Samantha. I wondered if there could be more than some coincidence but couldn't see how. So I agreed to meet up with Emma for a stake-out of the park, deciding to keep the police out of it for now, hoping to finally have something tangible to take to DS Black.

I arrived first, with the evening's chill on my face and a sense of déjà-vu, sitting on the agreed bench, a discreet distance from where the woman reported seeing the girl. Opposite me, at the other end of the park, three girls and a boy played, split between the swings and the slide, shuttling back and forth. I marvelled at their energy, their unselfconscious abandon, wondering back to my own childhood and trying to identify when the change had come, when wonder had become fear, when carefree had become couldn't care less. As I watched I couldn't help feel how vulnerable they were, so tiny and 'portable' for any monster hidden in plain sight. The lightness of their freedom, the darkness that hid in the shadows, the heavy responsibility of parenthood, the-

"Jesus fuck!"

I hadn't heard Emma as she approached, finally sensing her presence only as she sat beside me.

"I see your keen sense of observation will be invaluable tonight, Mr Holmes."

"I nearly fucking shit myself, Emma. You might have-"

"Gave you a warning? Not really up on this surveillance thing, are you?"

I smiled. "Shut up."

"See anything?"

"I'm not long here. Where exactly was it you said she saw her?"

Emma pointed. "Over there at the swing park then, when she looked back, she thought she saw her going into the bushes."

"Okay, so we just…"

"Sit and wait."

"Okay, I can do that. Do you still think we were right not to tell DS Black? I do but I-"

"Quietly, Tom."

So we sat and we waited, quietly.

On the outside at least. Outside my eyes were locked like a bird of prey on the other end of the park, scanning for the slightest movement or giveaway rustle. Inside my focus was less narrow. What were the chances of the girl being Mary? It wasn't as if her appearance is extraordinary. Should I tell Emma about Fred? About the murder plot? Was I fucking nuts!? Her perfume smelt nice. I breathed in deeper to smell it hoping she wouldn't notice. I wondered if she still did that thing or whether that was just ours. How could Mary have been gone so long, unnoticed while so close? But what if she had and it really was her?

"Do you think it could have been her?" I whispered.

"There's always a chance."

That's why I'd loved Emma. She'd always been so positive and hopeful. Full of belief, even in someone like me who was everything she wasn't. Maybe opposites attract, but it took more strength than I had to keep her. I did wonder sometimes if I had been more of a case than anything else. Someone to fix. But broken as I was, there was more, or there could have been if I'd spoken to her. Not too proud to ask for help. Fuck all to be proud of now, Tom. Maybe it wasn't too late, but not now: now was not the time for passes. I bet she just did that thing with me, though.

I shivered as the breeze whipped up, quietly rubbing my hands together, looking at my watch as I did. Nine. I hadn't even noticed the light slip quietly away, as if it too feared the dark.

"Maybe we have more chance of seeing her move in the dark."

"I think so. Maybe she's nocturnal. Safer. Fewer people about."

"What time did the woman see her?" I asked.

"I can't remember. Daytime though. Maybe she just got fed up. Can you imagine her life?"

"Not really."

I'd tried not to. I'd tried not to think of the pain she'd run from, or the merciless existence she now endured. Instead I hung only to the fairytale ending, her safe return to parents who'd lost all hope, and to justice for the culprits. Legal or vigilante, it made no difference now.

Midnight

One a.m.

Two a.m.

Three a.m.

"Maybe we should look in the bushes, Emma? She might be sleeping."

"Okay. I thought she'd have been out by now. I don't know how she lives like this."

"If it's her."

"I think it is, Tom. Call it instinct or whatever you want. It's her."

We got up and walked down quietly across the grass, listening and watching for movement in the darkness. Soon we were at the bushes. I searched for an easy way in. There wasn't one. But that was the point.

"I think I'm going to have to crawl."

"Okay. Can you smell it?"

"Yeah. Smells like dog shit. I'll watch where I put my hands."

I got down on all fours, pushing branches aside as I forced my way inside the outer barrier. Inside it was easier, less resistance but dirtier and the smell grew worse as I worked my way in. I could see the wall, the end of the line. Then I saw the packets, empty, but not litter, there was a sense of order. I could now see the shit, further along. I looked away instinctively, feeling a violation of privacy. In doing so I saw the remnants of food supplies, some spoiled, waiting for Mary. But I sensed she wouldn't be back.

I crawled back out stretching to full height.

"Well?"

"She's been there, Emma. I'm sure of it. There's food…She's been there. Lived in that bush for Christ knows how long. But she's gone, and I don't think she'll be coming back."

"Maybe the woman scared her off."

"Yeah, maybe."

"But she's alive."

"I think she is, Emma. I really fucking think so."

Without thinking I hugged her.

When tomorrow came my mind still soared with an excitement thought lost with my belief in Santa. But now I felt my gift was being wrapped, its delivery assured and, like the three-year-old me, I got up after two hour's sleep with no trace of fatigue and no patience for waiting. Now, with the sense that I finally had something tangible, an area to focus on rather than the whole fucking world, I almost flew through the door leaving those scum behind for now until Mary and I returned to gate-crash their sick little baby shower.

CHAPTER 30

Billy stood outside the shop window, ignoring for now the dazzling array of second hand treasures best placed to tempt both the poor and the charitable inside. His gaze lay elsewhere, fixed on the face reflected by the glass, its bushy brown hair pulled back as tightly as his numb, stubby fingers could manage and held in place by elastic bands, their rubber perished but holding for now. He knew how they felt. While his hair had been offered a semblance of neatness and order, if not respectability, his beard, a friend in winter, nuisance at mealtimes and disguise at all times, would have to remain a brown, ginger and grey wilderness. Besides, his clothes were enough to reflect all there was to see, in the eyes of the world at least.

Although his choice of mirror had been completely random, Fate's choice did get his mind to thinking as he looked past his reflection, through to the racks of second hand clothes, hanging clean, neat and tidy. He decided to take a look, feeling the warmth wrap him as he entered, before a cold front hit. It came with looks rather than words at first. Ignoring it, Billy flicked through the suits and coats hanging like limp cadavers, or the mortal remains of such. Tweed and polyester, lapels large and larger, forced into

215

neighbourliness by death, commerce and the Presbyterian eye for style. But for Billy the only criteria were warmth and a short cut to respectability, or at least enough of it for what came next. A heavy Parka held some promise, looking warm, clean and of the current decade. He looked at the price tag. Five pounds seemed reasonable, albeit for a luxury he could ill afford.

"Can I help you?"

Billy sighed. "Jist looking, thanks." A phrase his wife had scattered like confetti on shopping assistants all those years ago. But this was now.

"Please don't touch the clothes if you're not buying."

He turned towards the voice wondering what its eyes held. Suspicion? Contempt? While he had been ready for those, he was unprepared for what now faced him. Fear. Unfathomable to Billy but there it was. Naked fear. He reached into his pocket searching for, then brandishing a five pound note, the ticket of admission to a world which would always exclude him, with even the redundant clothes of the dead too good for the likes of Billy. He searched her eyes for pity or even guilt, but fear held firm even as he made towards the door, Parka-less.

Outside, the bitter winds welcomed him home and he headed for the chemist down at the end of the road. A small independent, it was normally quiet and the pharmacist was an old friend. As he entered the mousy girl at the counter glanced up with a familiar look, Billy by now no longer caring.

"Is Malcolm in?"

"Who shall I say-"

"Tell him it's Billy."

"Billy wh-"

"Jist Billy, " he snapped. "He'll know."

She turned and scuttled nervously to the adjoining office, closing the door behind her. Billy looked around aimlessly, scanning the well-stocked shelves while knowing what he needed was not to be found there. A head appeared around the partition wall, obviously not liking what it saw.

"I thought…"

"I know. Got a minute? It's important."

Malcolm nodded for Billy to come through. The girl kept her distance as Billy passed her, eyes focused attentively on anywhere else. Billy closed the door behind him and sat down on the black, hard-backed chair. Opposite him Malcolm just shrugged.

"Ah need yur help," said Billy firmly.

"I don't give that sort of help anymore."

"It's no-"

"If I dish out so much as a Cocodamol without a prescription, I'm fucked."

"It's no fur me."

"Yeah, right. I don't care who it's for."

"We've been mates a long time, Malky."

"We *were* mates a long time ago, Billy. There's a difference."

"Aye, the old days, eh? Me n you. Remember school?"

"Fuck's sake, Billy. You're going back a bit there."

"How many kickings did ah stoap you from getting? You and yer smart-arse wee mooth. Hunners? Mair?"

"Like I said, Billy. That was-"

"Then when you were the borin cunt at uni, who got yae rode?"

"And the clap. Three fucking times."

"Beggars n choosers, Malky. Which brings us nicely to Malky the young…What's the word? Dispensing chemist. Aye, that's it. And very happy to dispense, I seem to remember."

"That was a long time ago."

"You were on yer arse, aboot tae go oot ae business. Who saved yae?"

"I was desperate."

"Who sent the customers your way?"

"Customers?"

"Aye, payin customers. You were happy to take thur money."

"Look Billy, as I've said a hundred times before, I'm grateful. I really am, but you were well looked after too. And we agreed-"

"I don't remember much ae an agreement. Mair you jist pulling the shutters doon."

"You know why. They were getting suspicious."

"Aye, the mythical 'they'."

"Fuck's sake, Billy. That sort of stuff gets scrutinized like you wouldn't believe."

"Ah never did. Ah still don't."

"Christ…Look, Billy, we had a good run but it couldn't go on forever. We both did well out of it, not just me. But it's in the past. I can't help you, Billy. Have you not thought about the methadone programme?"

"Et tu Malky?"

"Eh?"

"You look at me and all you see is a junkie."

Billy sat passively allowing his old friend to look him over, examine, judge.

"Well? Whit dae yae see then?"

"You've looked better, Billy."

Billy smiled. "Ah'll gi yae that. But this is jist the street. Ah've no touched the gear fur years. Four years, five months tae be precise."

"So…What is it you want, mate?"

"Mate? Been a while since ah heard that word. But ah am, Malky. Even now. Even looking like this. Ah wis proud e ye when ye went to Uni. Even prouder when ye opened this place. It wisnae aw aboot getting stuff. It wis pride tae. In you, how well ye'd done and that ah could help ye."

"I know, Billy." Malcolm smiled sadly and reached over, putting his hand on Billy's arm. "Do you ever see…"

"Na. Better aff without me."

"But if you're clean."

"Ah jist don't know if ah could handle that life. Ah couldnae let her see me like this. It's no fair oan hur. She'd be embarrassed and nae wonder. Ah couldnae handle that. That look in her face. Naw, she's better aff."

"Maybe some day, eh?"

"Aye, maybe…someday."

Malcom sat back, shrugging once more.

"So, if it's not…What is it you want from me?"

"Something for flu, a chest infection, burnin temperature."

"Seriously?"

"Aye."

"You want medicine?"

"Aye."

"Why don't they just go to the doctor's?"

"She's…They're no registered."

"They'll still-"

"Yae jist huv tae trust me. Can yae jist gae is somethin."

"Why not just buy some Paracetamol."

"It's worse than that, Malky. Much worse."

The look in Billy's eye was all the convincing Malcolm needed. "So take them to hospital?"

"Na, that's no really…"

"You said she."

"Did ah?"

"Yes. Is she a girlfriend?"

"Fuck, naw."

"How old is she?"

"Whit diz that maiter?"

"Different medicines for different ages."

220

Billy felt the claustrophobia of the old straight world and its scrutiny start to choke him but knew he couldn't leave without what he came for.

"Listen, Malky, ah jist need ye tae trust me. For auld time's sake, can ye do that? Please."

They both sat in a brief moment of quiet, waiting for sentiment to dissolve suspicion.

"Sounds like they need an antibiotic. I'll give you one that's okay for any age. She'll need to finish the course."

"I'll make sure they do. Disnae sleep too good either."

"Rest's important but I'm not dishing out sleeping pills to chil…" Malcolm sighed and shook his head. "Night Nurse is as good as anything. Just between you and me it's what I use when I can't get to sleep. But it's got Paracetamol in it so don't mix it and only give her it at night. I'll give you something to help with the cough too, till the antibiotic starts to work."

"I give her Paracetemol for pain, but it doesnae-"

"I can't give you, her, anything stronger. Like I said, they're all over that stuff, Billy."

"You've done enough. The pain'll go when the other stuff works anywae, eh?"

"Should do."

"Ah really appreciate this. Sure you'll no get intae trouble?"

"A few antibiotics are fine. It's…You know."

"Aye, the good stuff."

They shared a grin and Malcolm stood up.

"Give me a minute. I'll get it for you."

True to his word he handed the packages over as the girl did her best to appear blissful in her ignorance.

"Bye, Billy."

"Bye, Malky."

He nodded to the girl, smiled and turned to leave. Then he saw it. The notice board and amongst the handyman ads and flats for rent, Mary's picture. He turned and looked back, his eyes meeting his friend's for what Billy knew would be the last time.

CHAPTER 31

Billy woke with the same feeling of disorientation into which every morning had delivered him since he'd left his family and responsibilities behind years before. Taking only the clothes he stood in, with anger and bitterness hidden in the pockets, he escaped to freedom on the streets but found only a mirage. For there was no freedom in chaos. The shifting sands on which his new life were founded instilled only fear in him. Firstly fear of the unknown and then fear of hostility. Then as hostility manifested, fear of violence, injury or worse. Finally, worst of all he'd been left with the ever-attentive fear of fear itself, knowing any random sight, sound or thought could trigger merciless waves of adrenalin to course through his body, an all-seeing, all-knowing enemy within, always one step ahead and against which he was powerless. He rubbed his eyes, pushing away the remnants of sleep, his body stretching to break free of itself before recognising it as folly as he looked around and remembered.

Beside him Carnation's inscrutable gaze met his own.

'Fuckin cat.'

"And how are you this morning, Carnation?" Billy reached over and stroked her ear.

"What's the matter, cat got your tongue?"

Beyond the cat in her rucksack palace, Billy heard Mary stir. He sat up and looked over at the tiny sweat-soaked figure, pain displayed in every struggle for movement. Her translucent eyelids hung closed, blending with the greyness of her face, coated in what looked more like slime than sweat. Billy did some arithmetic then groped around in his coat pocket until he found what he was looking for. He checked the packet. Day six of the antibiotics. Day six of a course of seven. He looked at her again now unable to lie or pretend to himself. Whatever happy ever after future he dreamed of was over. She was dying in front of his eyes.

"Mary."

"Mmmm."

"Mary, are ye awake?"

Another moan.

"Ye need tae go tae hospital."

Fear seemed to inject some of its energy into her.

"No I…"

"You're really no well, Mary."

"Carnation."

Billy turned to the toy then back to Mary.

"You huv tae believe me, Mary. We need tae get ye intae hospital, now."

"He's right, Mary. You…"

But Carnation couldn't say the words.

Mary nodded almost imperceptibly. "Okay, Carnation."

224

Without thinking Billy stroked the cat's ear again.

"She's a true pal, Mary."

"Told you."

He smiled the saddest smile and lay his hand on her head unchallenged. She smiled back.

"That's what Dad used to do when I wasn't well."

Billy's tears ran freely through the creases and the dirt, soaking his beard with their sweet pain.

"Ah need tae leave ye tae get help, bit ah'll be right back, my Mary. Right back."

He struggled to his feet and looked down at her, hating to leave, wondering what he'd find on his return, before rushing out into the sunlight to search for help in the world of strangers.

Billy returned quickly, lowering himself gently beside her and taking her hand.

"Billy?"

"Yes, Mary?"

"Am I going to die?"

"You're no g-"

"Carnation says I might."

"You're no goin tae die."

"I don't mind."

Billy stroked her hand softly.

"Do you think they have macaroni in Heaven?"

"Don't you worry aboot that."

"I think they will. I think it'll be hot. With chips too."

"And tomato sauce."

"And tomato sauce. A big squeezy bottle. Heinz."

"Only the best for my Mary."

Then they just sat, waiting, Billy wiping her brow, Mary smiling. Carnation silent.

"I think that's the ambulance."

"Okay."

Two men appeared in the darkness stumbling into a hidden world, medical missionaries among the lost and the destitute.

"Jesus," said the first.

The second just looked, first at Mary, then Billy. He spoke no words as his eyes seared guilt into Billy's soul.

Billy watched as the paramedics gently lifted her, following behind uncertainly as they carried her to the ambulance.

"Are you coming?" asked one.

"Aye," was all Billy said, climbing in, staying close.

As they drove, Billy reached into his pocket, taking out a piece of paper, neatly folded. He opened it to reveal Mary as she once was, so young and healthy but with a look in her eye maybe only he understood. His attention turned to the phone number beneath.

"Do they have phones at the hospital?"

"Payphones."

His hand dipped back into his pocket, fingers silently identifying each coin, counting. He had enough.

226

CHAPTER 32

There was a time that any unrecognised number would be ignored or acknowledged only with a muttered "Fuck off". But now my contact with the world had expanded past PPI claims and accidents I'd never had. I looked at the screen, welcoming this stranger as a gambler welcomes the spin of the roulette wheel.

"Hello."

The voice answered with a low, nervous rasp. But the words were clear enough.

"You the guy lookin fur the wee lassie?"

I felt sick, not quite able to believe what I'd heard.

"Who are you?"

"That disnae matter. Is it you?"

"Yes."

"So who are ye? Why ye lookin fur hur?"

"How do I know that you-"

"Her name's Mary. What's she tae you?"

I'd kept her name off the poster for this very reason. To sort out the time wasters and 'jokers'. Now it was me under the spotlight. I could hear the desperation in his voice, his need for me to be on his side, to trust me. So I repaid him with the truth.

"I've never met her. I just moved into her old house and saw her name written on a wall. I asked around about her. I don't really know why. Look, the short version is I think she was being abused by a neighbour. I just want to bring her home safe to her parents, whom I've also never met and who don't even know I'm doing this. I just-

"She's at the Southern General."

"What's the-"

"Get there," he said, voice scraped raw with a pain I recognised. "Get there quick."

He hung up. I stared at the phone until his last word echoed from my mouth.

"Quick!"

My thumb dials for a taxi as this was no time for apps. A woman's voice speaks. 'Urgently', I hear my voice say after I've given all necessary details. There seems to be a panic in it which now spreads to the rest of me. I go out to the street to wait, pacing back and forth. I think I locked the door. Doesn't seem to matter. A few minutes later I'm in the back of a car making small talk with the back of a stranger's head. I think it was a man, can't really remember. I just remember telling him to hurry and anger when he asks where the fire was. I nearly forget to pay him. It was a man, I remember now. Gave him twenty for a five quid fare. Told him to keep it, turned and ran.

That was about three weeks ago now. Three weeks since I'd found her.

CHAPTER 33

As I stood reading the words I found no comfort in their familiarity. Those words that had brought us together now the words that tore us apart.

Mary McDonald

Aged 11

Beloved daughter

I looked over at her parents, her father broken, only his responsibility to Mary's mother keeping him standing, his arm tight around her waist, pulling her close as her wounded moans and tears filled the earth to which she now entrusted her daughter's body for safe-keeping.

They say it's better to know than to spend a lifetime wondering. I saw no sign of that on that greyest of afternoons and, with her evidence following Mary to the grave, her mother and father's desperate, 'Where?' had merely been replaced by the equally cruel, 'Who? and 'Why?'

As for me, well, I'd gone to the police, or DS Black at least, and told him my story. Everything. All that she and Fred had revealed and my own stupidity in it all. But other than quieting my own conscience it was all for nothing. "No evidence, no case" was still Simon's anguished assessment. I sensed his anger, his frustration with the rules that bound him. I shared them, or at least the former.

The only comfort came from his promise that he'd pepper the system with more red flags than China and the adoption would happen over his dead body. It was something, but it wasn't enough.

I felt Emma's hand squeeze my own, feeling some comfort in that familiarity at least. It had been her company alone that had somehow managed to keep me sane in the hours and days since I'd lost Mary. Whether we had a future only the future knew, but it was here that I needed her and it was here she was. Someone who understood. Someone to talk to.

To my other side was Sylvia, her face carved with the share she claimed for herself, of the guilt, the failure, of hindsight, of 'should have'. I put my arm around her, a crumb of comfort for two starving souls.

At the police station, DS Black pushed back in his chair wishing it was the seventies when he could have opened up his bottom drawer, poured himself a large scotch and lit a cigarette, but these were more 'civilised' times, though the clear plastic bag on his desk begged to differ. There was nothing civilised about the dirt and neglect engrained on a child's clothing and no amount of green tea or decaffeinated lattes would make them smell any better or change their worn out, whimpering story.

The young cadet who'd joined the force to be Scotland's own Captain America, now, all these years later, felt as bitter and bleak as Batman but

230

with no cowl to hide his own sense of utter failure and defeat. He'd decided to stay away from Mary's funeral, hiding behind work to avoid the eyes of her parents. Besides, he was the last person they'd want to see. He'd failed them then, even questioning them as suspects, however briefly. And he'd failed them now. He had nothing for them. No case, no one in the dock to pay. So here he hid with the remnants of their daughter's last days.

He emptied the bag and spread the contents on his desk with a muttered, "Fuck forensics," scrutinizing each item for some missed detail, searching each pocket and crevice in her rucksack for even a crumb of a clue. Nothing. And that was it. A whole life, short as it was, reduced to nothing, or almost nothing. He picked up the stuffed cat, her sole companion for two years. He almost felt grateful to it for ensuring that Mary had never been quite alone, that she'd had 'someone' to talk to, even if they couldn't talk back. But it was scant comfort. He felt his anger build as he held the toy tight in his grip, ragged and dirty. A toy cat with a fucking wonky eye. He squeezed tighter, ready to hurl it against the wall…and then he saw it.

As Simon looked closer at the eye, he recognised it as the same camera lens his colleagues used on surveillance, albeit in a very different housing. He body-searched Carnation until he found what he was looking for and then, heart in mouth and SD card between thumb and index finger, he transferred it to his laptop. His adrenaline spiked as Mary suddenly appeared on the screen in what Simon remembered as her bedroom. He gasped as she picked up the camera, seeming to look right through it, directly into his own eyes before talking to him. But even in the absence of sound he quickly realised it was the toy she was speaking to, kissing it before the screen went black with a hug.

He quickly skipped through the footage of a child alone in her room, watching TV, doing homework, a kiss goodnight from her dad. Then he appeared. Fred, his face closing in on the camera as he picked it up, moving it from place to place until he had the view he wanted. A view of Mary's bed. He then turned to the bedroom door, appearing to shout before another figure appeared, a woman and in her outstretched hand, the hand of a child. As she brought Mary into the room, Samantha's face looked around until she found it, smiling at the camera and DS Black. He watched the rest knowing he would never be the same.

As the minister droned on about the mysteries of life and death I looked across the grave at the creatures who had dug it. Fred and his accomplice stood bold as brass, their faces solemn but with a smirk in their eyes only I could see. I felt my phone buzz once. Given the circumstances I should have ignored it. I glanced down and saw the words 'DS Black'. I clicked on the message.

232

'Tom, the cat was a camera. Took video of Fred with Mary. Bitch is in the background too. Uniform on way. We've got the fuckers, Tom!!'

I kept my eyes fixed on the ground, straining to compose myself lest I give the game away too soon. Looking into the grave as they lowered Mary in, I wanted to scream in after her that I was sorry, but that they would suffer now as she had.

I felt my body shake as I finally looked up. She saw me and smiled. But as our eyes met I held Samantha's gaze tight, and with a smile of my own, smashed those windows to whatever soul she had until she knew. I watched the colour drain from her face, the slight buckle in her legs, the sideways look to Fred…and the police uniforms as they approached.

Back at the station Carnation softly purred one last time.

THE END

Hi. I hope you enjoyed the book. If you did, I'd really appreciate it if you could spare a few moments to leave a short review on Amazon or wherever you purchased it. It really makes a HUGE difference. Thanks!

ALSO BY ROBERT COWAN:

THE SEARCH FOR ETHAN
DAYDREAMS AND DEVILS
FOR ALL IS VANITY
FIRM

WEBSITE:
https://www.robertcowanbooks.wordpress.com
FACEBOOK: @robertcowanwriter
TWITTER: @robcow63

Printed in Great Britain
by Amazon

69087106R00144